## *What was that?*

Nothing moved. Even the wind was still. Only the water flowed over the rocks, bubbling in a way that would be soothing and peaceful...if Kelsie wasn't staring at an abandoned shovel, a rectangular dig site and a horrifyingly human-shaped bundle wrapped in thick plastic and bound with duct tape.

Adrenaline and nausea threw a one-two punch to her gut.

Someone was burying a body...and she'd interrupted them.

Warm sweat mingled with cool mist on her skin. Someone had been here when she drove up. Someone who had already killed once.

Her muscles tensed. Her head pounded. Where were they hiding?

The shadows could conceal anyone. The darkness was coming. She would fight, though, and she would win. This time, no one would catch her off—

A car door slammed.

Kelsie whirled toward her vehicle, out of sight through the trees. Was that her car? Or had someone else—

But before she could turn, a force slammed into the small of her back...driving her to the ground.

**Jodie Bailey** is a *New York Times, USA TODAY* and *Publishers Weekly* bestselling author who writes "soul-stirring suspense" filled with love, faith and intrigue. Her novel *Crossfire* was an RT Reviewers' Choice Best Book Award winner that was commended for addressing "the stigma associated with mental health services and the military." She is a mom and army wife who believes dark chocolate cures all ills. She lives in North Carolina with her husband and a Lab-husky mix.

## Books by Jodie Bailey

### Love Inspired Suspense

*Captured at Christmas*
*Witness in Peril*
*Blown Cover*
*Deadly Vengeance*
*Undercover Colorado Conspiracy*
*Hidden in the Canyon*

### Trinity Investigative Team

*Taken at Christmas*
*Protecting the Orphan*
*Buried Mountain Justice*

### Pacific Northwest K-9 Unit

*Olympic Mountain Pursuit*

### Mountain Country K-9 Unit

*Montana Abduction Rescue*

### Dakota K-9 Unit

*Tracing Killer Evidence*

Visit the Author Profile page at LoveInspired.com for more titles.

# BURIED MOUNTAIN JUSTICE

## JODIE BAILEY

If you purchased this book without a cover you should be aware that this book is stolen property. It was reported as "unsold and destroyed" to the publisher, and neither the author nor the publisher has received any payment for this "stripped book."

**LOVE INSPIRED® SUSPENSE**
INSPIRATIONAL ROMANCE

ISBN-13: 978-1-335-90646-5

Buried Mountain Justice

Copyright © 2025 by Jodie Bailey

All rights reserved. No part of this book may be used or reproduced in any manner whatsoever without written permission.

Without limiting the exclusive rights of any author, contributor or the publisher of this publication, any unauthorized use of this publication to train generative artificial intelligence (AI) technologies is expressly prohibited. Harlequin also exercises their rights under Article 4(3) of the Digital Single Market Directive 2019/790 and expressly reserves this publication from the text and data mining exception.

This is a work of fiction. Names, characters, places and incidents are either the product of the author's imagination or are used fictitiously. Any resemblance to actual persons, living or dead, businesses, companies, events or locales is entirely coincidental.

For questions and comments about the quality of this book, please contact us at CustomerService@Harlequin.com.

® is a trademark of Harlequin Enterprises ULC.

| Love Inspired | HarperCollins Publishers |
|---|---|
| 22 Adelaide St. West, 41st Floor | Macken House, 39/40 Mayor Street Upper, |
| Toronto, Ontario M5H 4E3, Canada | Dublin 1, D01 C9W8, Ireland |
| www.LoveInspired.com | www.HarperCollins.com |

**Printed in U.S.A.**

But as for you, ye thought evil against me; but God meant it unto good, to bring to pass, as it is this day, to save much people alive.
—*Genesis* 50:20

To Elise,

I love you, and I'm so glad we're family...

Even if you did read my book in front of me on the beach

# ONE

Nothing good could come of being this close to home.

Even this investigation was starting out wrong. Kelsie McIlheney ended her call when it went to voicemail. She stared at a sky heavy with clouds. Mist hung in the winter mountain air, clinging to her clothes and face.

Hot annoyance prickled her skin. She was supposed to meet a special agent with the Virginia State Police Bureau of Criminal Investigation to walk through an old crime scene, but the woman was an hour late, and she wasn't answering her phone. Worse, the device seemed to be turned off.

Either Special Agent Anna Whitmire had found the longest dead zone in the Appalachians, or she was ignoring Kelsie's phone calls.

But why?

Glancing at her phone to check the time, Kelsie leaned against the driver's door of her SUV and looked up the dirt track she'd followed across a field near the perimeter of Burke's Garden, Virginia.

The field sat near the slope of what, from above, looked like an eight-mile-long volcanic crater. Visiting the area required a twisting drive along a narrow two-lane road that wound up, over and back down the mountains that ringed the large natural bowl.

About three hundred people lived a relatively quiet existence in Burke's Garden. At times, ice and snow isolated residents, including several Amish families, from the outside world. They were content to remain in the small community with a couple of general stores, a school, and an abundance of farmland and cattle.

The area's remoteness made the tucked-away grove of trees before her the perfect place to bury a body. Hidden. Quiet. Away from prying eyes.

Five years earlier, someone had done just that. It had been a fluke that a farmer had found the remains of Elias Moore, his makeshift grave partially exposed after a historic rainfall caused the creek to rise. The violence had rocked the small community.

Thoughts of buried bodies, winding roads and darkness shivered up Kelsie's spine.

If she was being honest, her uneasiness had nothing to do with irritation or isolation.

No, it was the memories. It was coming back to the Virginia mountains for the first time in sixteen years. It was facing the nightmare she'd fought so hard to overcome.

Kelsie rolled her head from one side to the other, tugged her coat's zipper higher, then looked at her phone again. Sunset wasn't far off. She could take care of herself, but she had no desire to prove it when night fell.

She needed to get out of here.

Punching her boss's contact on her cell, she raised the phone to her ear. Elliott Weiss didn't know it, but he'd asked a lot of her when he'd assigned this case. Sure, Kelsie had decided it was time to prove to herself that she was strong enough to stand up to the past, but she blamed her uncharacteristic nerves on Elliott for suggesting the trip in the first place.

He answered on the second ring. "Find anything interesting?"

"Haven't looked. Do you have another number for Special Agent Whitmire? Her phone goes straight to voicemail. She's an hour late, and it'll be dark soon."

Darkness was never her friend.

Not that she'd tell Elliott. He was the hard-charging former Special Forces soldier who'd founded Trinity Investigations seven years earlier. Very little rattled him, unless one of his team was in trouble.

"You're in the mountains. She could have spotty service." Road noise in the background said Elliott was driving somewhere, probably to Pamlico Correctional Institution to hold another interview with an informant in the murder of Keith Galloway, another case Trinity was looking into.

A personal case.

Maybe Elliott was right, but something felt off. She'd chatted with Special Agent Whitmire a couple of hours earlier to confirm their meetup. Everything had been a go.

"Don't be in such a hurry. You rolled into town ninety minutes ago. It's going to take a week or so to review this case, right? You've got files to go over and witnesses to talk to. If you don't see the crime scene today, you'll see it tomorrow. I already told you—"

"I know, I know." He'd told her to go straight to her short-term rental about half an hour from Burke's Garden and to take the evening to get situated before she jumped into the case, but she really wanted to get this done and get out.

Her need to get moving wasn't *entirely* personal. The quicker she wrapped up her reinvestigation, the quicker state prosecutors could finalize their strategies for the retrial of convicted murderer Trenton Daniels. When the defense requested a retrial based on mishandled evidence, the state had asked Trinity to trace the original investigation from start to finish to ensure there had been no issues.

Trinity specialized in looking back through

cases for prosecutors or defense attorneys in order to spot inconsistencies or uncover missed evidence. Given that Daniels's victim, Elias Moore, had been a well-known attorney a couple of counties over, the murder had made headlines. The state wanted to be certain they had done everything right the first time and had missed nothing.

Her phone buzzed, and she glanced at the screen to find an unknown number. Filling in for Special Agent Whitmire. On my way.

She puffed out a breath. No ETA. No name. No respect.

"What was that sigh?" As usual, Elliott missed nothing.

"Whitmire isn't showing. She's sent a pinch hitter."

"You going to stand by?"

"No. I've wasted more time than I wanted to. I'm going in by myself. If I have questions, I'll save them for her stand-in. It's not like we *need* them. I have the landowner's permission to be here. Reaching out to Virginia was a professional courtesy."

She needed to be done with this. Driving through Hillandale County and past the Shiloh Peak exit on I-77 had been harder than she'd imagined. There was nothing for her in the Virginia mountains except fractured memories best left buried.

"We also wanted help pinpointing the exact location of the burial site. The file was a bit vague." Elliott wasn't going to let this go.

But he couldn't trip her up. She'd studied the case files, and it wasn't as *vague* as he thought. "Fifty-two yards in from the north, thirty-four yards in from the east, beneath a V-shaped dogwood tree. What else ya got?" She shoved away from the SUV. The only way she'd get through this would be through sarcasm and false bravado, her weapons of choice.

Elliott chuckled. "I know better than to tell you *no*. Odds are you won't stumble on anything that hasn't already been uncovered. You're there to get a feel for the place so when you're reading case files or talking to witnesses, you can fill in the gaps."

"Roger, boss." She killed the call and pocketed her phone before he could dole out more sage advice she'd already heard a thousand times. He gave the speech every time.

Kelsie moved toward the wood line, making a quick scan of the overcast sky. The sun was headed for the horizon behind the low-hanging clouds, and the shadows among the trees sank into deep pools of darkness.

Kelsie stopped halfway between her car and the trees, standing in ankle-high dried grass. Then air felt stirred, as though something unseen was passing through.

Maybe she should have taken her pistol out of its locked box beneath her front seat.

But no. It was too late in the year for snakes and, while bears might not be hibernating, they were certainly sluggish and indulging in extra-long naps.

The odds of anyone lying in wait for her were practically zero. There was only one good paved road into Burke's Garden, and even it could get iffy in the winter months. The secondary gravel back road would be virtually impassable given the recent cold, wet weather, and a nearby dirt road was little more than a trail.

She'd be safe despite the deepening shadows.

Counting her steps, she made her way in the general direction the case file had noted, hanging a right when she'd paced off approximately fifty-two yards. A few more steps and she was standing in sight of a V-shaped dogwood, where Trenton Daniels had buried Elias Moore's remains.

She circled the spot, taking in the vegetation and the general feel of the area. It had been five years since a flooding creek had partially revealed Elias Moore's final resting place.

Although the scene had been swept by multiple agencies when the remains were discovered, it never hurt to look again.

Kelsie wandered through the trees toward the creek, making note of the topography and snapping a few photos to keep images strong in her mind. It was possible subsequent flooding had uncovered more evidence although, as Elliott had said, the chances were low.

One time, though, fellow Trinity investigator Hayden McGrath had discovered—

*What was that?* Her feet slid to a stop on damp leaves.

Her heart picked up the pace. Surely she wasn't seeing what her eyes said she was seeing.

Slowly, Kelsie pocketed her phone so both hands would be free, carefully surveying the banks of the shallow creek.

Nothing moved. Even the air was still. Only the water flowed over the rocks, bubbling in a way that would be soothing and peaceful...

...if she wasn't staring at an abandoned shovel, a rectangular dig site and a horrifyingly human-shaped bundle wrapped in thick plastic and bound with duct tape.

Adrenaline and nausea threw a one-two punch to her gut.

Someone was burying a body, and she'd interrupted them.

Measuring her breaths and forcing herself to remain quiet, Kelsie backed away, attempting to retrace her steps so she wouldn't further disturb potential evidence on the way out.

Warm sweat mingled with cool mist on her skin. Someone had been here when she drove up. Someone who had already killed once.

Her muscles tensed. Her head pounded. Where were they hiding?

The shadows could conceal anyone. The darkness was coming. She would fight, though, and she would win. This time, no one would catch her off—

A car door slammed.

Kelsie whirled toward her vehicle, out of sight through the trees. Was that her car? Or had someone else—

A rustling came from behind her. Before she could turn, a force slammed into the small of her back, driving her to the ground.

Special Agent Noah Cross tugged on his gloves to ward off the January chill, then he stepped out of his unmarked SUV and rolled his eyes toward the clouds, wishing he was home where he should be. The misty rain was so much worse than dry cold. The clouds hinted snow was headed their way, and he'd really like to be on the other side of the mountain before it decided to drop. The only paved road into Burke's Garden could get dicey quick.

This wasn't supposed to be his job. Anna Whitmire had been the lead agent on the Moore murder and had agreed to meet with the out-of-town independent investigator. When the case had been investigated initially, Noah had been working at a field office near the coast. An opening in Hillandale County had brought him closer to home less than a year earlier, so he wasn't entirely familiar with the case.

A frantic phone call from Special Agent Whitmire's husband had changed his afternoon plans. She'd gone into labor a week early, and they were headed to the hospital.

That left Noah to meet this Trinity Investigations person.

The whole thing felt like an exercise in futility. Despite the request for a retrial, he was certain the original case had been solid. While he hadn't worked that particular crime, he knew the agents with the Virginia State Police Violent Crimes Unit had done their due diligence. Along with forensic techs and local law enforcement, their work had undoubtedly been thorough, especially given the high-profile nature of the murder. An out-of-state private investigator wasn't going to find anything they'd done wrong.

He resented the implication that the Bureau of Criminal Investigation needed follow-up. Yeah, they were from one of the poorest regions in the state, but they weren't slouches. They were a top-notch group, as well-trained as those jokers in the larger cities who had requested this "reinvestigation."

Stalking to the dark blue SUV with out-of-state tags, he knocked on the front window then peered inside.

Empty.

Of course, the outsider had taken matters into his own hands. The guy obviously didn't need his help. Maybe he should—

A sharp cry cut off abruptly and was quickly followed by a dull thud.

Noah stepped toward the wooded area where Trenton Daniels had buried Elias Moore five years earlier. Had the investigator fallen into the icy creek? Winter had been unusually mild for the area, but even "warm" was colder than most people liked.

Noah smirked. Wouldn't that be—

Another cry, this one angry and forceful, was followed by another thud.

That wasn't a fall.

That was a fight.

He took off running, his hand hovering over his service weapon at his hip.

He crashed through the trees like a bear on the hunt. As he entered a small clearing near the creek, two figures came into view.

A person knelt on one knee, clothed in what looked like bulky gray mechanic's coveralls, their face covered in a ski mask. It was tough to discern gender given the clothing and the stance.

The figure jumped to its feet as Noah approached, though they didn't appear to see him.

The second person, a female dressed in jeans and a thick navy blue windbreaker, had her back to Noah. She raised their hands in an offensive posture, clearly ready to carry on the fight. "What else have you got?" Her voice held an angry challenge, and her dark ponytail swung where it had been pulled through the back of a tan baseball cap.

Before he could call out, the person in coveralls lunged, but the woman was ready. With a roundhouse kick worthy of any old-school Bruce Lee movie, her heel cracked into her opponent's jaw. She moved with a lethal grace that snagged something in Noah's memory.

Her opponent staggered into a tree, barely managing to remain upright.

The woman advanced, taking the offensive position. "Give up."

Enough was enough. "State police! Both of you stand down!" He unclipped his holster, but he didn't draw his Sig. Neither of the subjects appeared to be armed, so hopefully whatever this was would deescalate with law enforcement on the scene.

Without turning, the woman lowered her hands, holding them slightly out to her sides. "I'm handling it."

*Handling what?* Before Noah could respond, the figure in coveralls bolted, splashing through the creek and disappearing into the shadowy trees on the other side. Before he could give chase, a small engine fired up and roared off, heading toward the gravel "back" road out of Burke's Garden.

"Are you kidding me?" The woman held her hands out wider, this time in exasperation. "I was about to hand you a killer."

*"A killer?"* What was she talking about? If she was the Trinity investigator, then she was trouble already. "I walked up on a fight, not a—"

"Good job, Officer." The woman bit off the word. "You detained the wrong person." She turned slowly. "That was—" Her gaze landed on his and she stopped, a statue frozen in time.

The most beautiful statue he'd ever seen.

Her blue eyes went wide. Her head tilted. Her lips parted...

...but she didn't speak.

Noah wasn't sure he could either.

There was no way this was real. His eyes said she was right there in front of him, but his mind refused to compute. "Kelsie?" Even as he said her name, he knew it couldn't be true. He was supposed to be meeting an investigator, not... Not a ballet dancer from his past who inexplicably had the skills of an MMA fighter in the present.

The Kelsie lookalike lowered her hands, and her gaze hardened. "You have a phone? You have the sheriff, the police, somebody on speed dial? Get them out to the main road so they can grab whoever blasted out of here."

Instinct drove him to obey, although the command made no sense coming from her...especially if she was his Kelsie.

No, not *his*. Not anymore.

But it was definitely her. Nothing had changed except for some seriously sharp edges to her formerly grace-filled personality.

He had his phone in his hand before he thought to ask questions. "Why am I stopping that person? Who are they?"

She simply pointed toward the creek.

Noah forgot everything else. Lying near the water was a large bundle wrapped in layers of opaque plastic and sealed tightly with duct tape. A shovel lay abandoned near a hole several feet across and at least a foot deep.

At some point along the trek from his SUV to the creek, he must have started hallucinating, because there was no way this scene was real.

The chill that ran up his spine said he wasn't dreaming. Someone had been burying a body.

Punching his phone screen, he made the call to dispatch.

It was probably fruitless. The engine had sounded like a Quadrunner or similar off-road vehicle. They could take any number of trails out or hide anywhere in Burke's Garden's forty-square miles.

Kelsie didn't move as he requested crime scene techs and a coroner.

Pocketing his phone, he forced himself to look at the woman in front of him, the woman he still couldn't believe he was seeing. *Work, Noah. You have work to do.* Their very broken past and all of his questions would have to wait. "This is about to be a very active crime scene." He barely managed to keep his voice from rattling with a thousand emotions. "We need to secure the area and step back."

She nodded and moved away, keeping her distance from him and her guard up. She stood ramrod straight, her hat and hair damp from the chilled mist. Her gaze never turned toward him.

Noah let her keep her space as he attempted to process what was happening.

He had a body in front of him and Kelsie McIlheney beside him...a woman he was convinced might have risen from the dead.

# TWO

"Then Special Agent Cross arrived." Kelsie addressed Noah's fellow agent as she settled her coffee on the desk in front of her. It was pure sugar, "brewed" out of a machine at the gas station.

At least it was caffeine.

After completing preliminaries at the scene, she found herself at the Hillandale County Sheriff's Office, the closest official building to Burke's Garden. There, state and local authorities were coordinating this new homicide investigation.

Kelsie had followed Special Agent Val Yewell along the dark, harrowing drive over the mountain. She'd white-knuckled every turn, her headlights barely cutting through the tree-thickened night.

Her brain was mush.

Her nerves were shot.

A body. A fight. The darkness.

*Noah.*

He should be in Virginia Beach, not anywhere near the mountains. She'd googled him before she took this assignment. Working a case within half an hour of her hometown would be hard enough without running headlong into the man she'd left behind.

The man who'd failed her.

If things went her way, she could get out of this office without having to see him again. She was already riding the edges of her emotional sanity.

Special Agent Yewell tapped her pen on the borrowed desk. While Noah remained at the crime scene, Yewell was taking Kelsie's statement. "You need a refill? I can send somebody to Brewed Awakening for you." She leaned closer with a smile in her green eyes. "It's better than whatever's in the break room."

"I heard that." One of the deputies smirked as he passed. "We can't help that Archer went to Europe on his honeymoon and decided coffee is better if your spoon stands up in it. Somebody let him near the machine before we could intervene." The tall, thin deputy stopped. "Also, you're out of luck. Brewed Awakening closed at five."

Good. She didn't want someone else bringing her coffee anyway, and she didn't want to have to explain why.

"Ms. McIlheney?" Agent Yewell leaned into Kelsie's line of sight, her forehead creased. "You weren't injured in the altercation, were you?"

Kelsie shook her head. *Not even close.* She'd worked hard to ensure she could defend herself against any adversary. Her teammates at Trinity liked to refer to her as *lethal*. She owned it. "It's been a long day, and it didn't go as expected." That was the definition of *understatement*.

"I'd imagine not." Yewell sat back and studied the pen in her hand. "You realize what happened today could have ramifications for the Daniels case."

Kelsie reeled in her wandering thoughts. She was here to do a job, and Noah crashing through the middle of it couldn't distract her. "If someone else is using that area as a dumping ground, it could create reasonable doubt and a stronger case for a retrial." The defense could argue the presence of a new burial site in the same remote location pointed to another killer utilizing the area.

"Possibly." It was clear Yewell didn't like the idea. Why would she? It placed an investigation her department had led in jeopardy. "Or it's a coincidence. We don't have a 'dumping ground' unless we find more remains."

"You can't rule out a copycat either. The location where Daniels buried Moore's remains was made public. It's also possible someone assumed that, since the original trial is long over, the area wouldn't be looked at again." A wave of weariness washed over her. There were too many things to consider, and this afternoon had been eleven days long. All she wanted was to pretend none of this had happened. She wanted a hot bath and a pity party.

Until tomorrow. Then she'd put on her big girl combat boots and do her job.

Kelsie stood and scanned the room, which was largely empty since most of the deputies in the small mountain community were on patrol. "I'm sure we'll talk again, Agent Yewell. For now, I'd like a decent meal." She was starving, and the brain fog was real. "Any suggestions?" Hillandale's Main Street was different than when she'd visited as a kid. The town had been dying then, but small shops and local restaurants now thrived in once-vacant storefronts.

"Call me Val." Special Agent Yewell stood and looked toward Main Street as though she could see through the walls. "Our field office is about half an hour from here, but I'm in Hillandale quite a bit. There's a deli a block up, or there's a noodle place with the best teriyaki chicken ever right across the street. If you're looking for something warm, I'd suggest the chicken on their mac and cheese. Sounds strange, but it tastes amazing."

It sounded amazing. Her mother had tried to break her of starchy, sugary foods when she was training as a ballet dancer, but the ban had never stuck. An afternoon in the damp chill confronting potential killers, dead bodies and nightmare memories screamed for comfort food. "Sounds perfect." Kelsie pulled her phone from her pocket and glanced at the address of her rental. "Any idea where the leather store is? I'm staying in a short-term apartment above it."

"Right across the parking lot." The voice over her shoulder was deep, familiar and totally unexpected.

Kelsie forced herself to turn slowly and not to throw a back kick.

*Noah.*

His hair was damp from the mist, and his navy overcoat was dark with moisture. His skin was nearly tinged blue from the steep temperature drop after sunset.

He surveyed her with deep brown eyes she'd never forgotten. A strand or two of gray weaved through his dark hair like tinsel, but it was only noticeable if she looked closely.

She shouldn't be looking closely.

His hand lifted as though he might reach out to her, but then it fell back to his side.

He did not need to touch her.

No one needed to touch her.

Oh, but for the briefest second, she wished he would. He'd once been her safe place when her parents asked for more than she could give, when she was exhausted from rehearsals, or when life wouldn't go the way she wanted. For two heartbeats, she missed the feel of his arms and the love they'd shared.

Noah had been her first love, her only love, but he hadn't been there when she needed him most.

Life would be so different if he had been.

Her mouth went dry at the flash of jolting awake in the dark, chilled and sick and terrified, the echo of a harsh whisper grating against her skull.

*Beautiful ballerina.*

She'd shed that title years ago, running from that moment. From that darkness. From that horror.

Nausea rocked her, and she grabbed the desk.

Concern darkened Noah's expression. "Are you okay?"

That night she'd taught herself to breathe through the fear, through the pain, through the unknown. The night she'd learned she could only count on herself.

Those lessons would save her now.

Commanding every ounce of reserves her exhausted body and emotions could muster, Kelsie found the mask she'd dropped and settled it over her features. She was a professional. She was a former soldier and a trained martial artist. She was a force to be reckoned with. "I'm perfectly fine."

She was also a liar.

"She was talking about being exhausted and hungry." Val rounded the desk and stood slightly in front of Kelsie. "This day has taken a toll on us all."

Noah studied Kelsie. "I can grab you something to eat if you—"

"I'm good." There was no way she was eating food she hadn't prepared or picked up herself. Ever.

Val watched them intently, tilting her head. "Noah, I've got a few more questions for Ms. McIlheney. If you want to get going, go ahead. I'll wrap up here if you want to head on out to Blue Heron."

Noah's eyes narrowed. It almost seemed as if he would refuse, but then he simply walked across the room and disappeared up a hallway. Anger wafted in his wake.

Kelsie was confused. Val had agreed they were done talking, hadn't she? What else could she have to ask?

She forced herself to stand tall when Val studied her as though she had the ability to read minds, but she felt exposed, as though all of her secrets were laid bare. There was no way this stranger could see her darkest memories, was there?

Feeling trapped wasn't a sensation she enjoyed. Neither was feeling as though she had no control.

And it was pretty clear Val held the control.

Well, she'd take it back. "What's Blue Heron?"

"The road he lives on. It's on the far side of the county." The other woman shoved her hands into her pockets, a posture that looked deliberately relaxed. "Do you know Detective Cross? I mean, did you before today?"

It took all of Kelsie's remaining energy to keep

her expression impassive. "We went to high school together." That was such a small sentence for what had been the closest relationship of her life, then or since. Noah had been the love of her life. Her best friend. Her confidant. Her safe place.

Until he hadn't been.

The truth still sliced like a rusty machete. She'd lost her life that night…including Noah.

Because she'd trusted everyone.

Val nodded slowly, her lips pursed as though she was deep in thought. "Is there something I should know? You seemed uncomfortable with his presence."

Kelsie shook her head, feeling as though she was fifteen and had been called into the principal's office.

But she wasn't the perpetrator. She was the—

*Victim.* She hated that word and had fought to wipe it from her very DNA. She'd served in the army, had faced down death and was more well-trained in martial arts than anyone else in this office, maybe even in this state. She answered to no one on personal matters. "If you have an issue with Special Agent Cross, then you should speak to him."

"No issue. Just curious."

She didn't owe this woman any further comment, but to keep silent would only create more questions. This little interview needed to end, and she needed to get out of here to a safe space behind locked doors. Apparently, said *safe space* was literally in the sheriff's backyard. "With all due respect, Special Agent Yewell, I found myself in an altercation with a possible murderer this afternoon. I'm a little jumpy. It has nothing to do with Special Agent Cross other than the way he snuck up on me like some kind of feral cat."

"I understand, and I told you to call me Val." Her smirk said she was biting back a laugh, though she sobered quickly. "Do you need anything else?"

"Dinner, and I can handle that. You can call me if you have any more questions."

"I'll pass that on to Detective Cross. He'll be taking lead." She glanced around the room as though Kelsie's response to Noah's involvement wasn't of interest to her. "Unless there's a problem?"

It was a huge problem, but there was no way she'd say so. "All good." She'd deal with Noah tomorrow. Today had delivered enough trouble.

After a terse goodbye, Kelsie stepped out into the damp, cold night. Sure enough, on the far side of the parking lot, smack in the center of a row of buildings, was a door that matched the one in the photos from the online listing.

That meant the noodle place was across a narrow side street, through deep shadows that crawled with a thousand memories. They slithered out of the darkness and up her spine, twisting until they paralyzed her. She almost choked on panic she hadn't felt in years.

She shouldn't have come here.

It was too close to home.

Too close to the darkness.

It was almost three in the morning. Noah's house was quiet and dim, the perfect conditions for sleep.

But sleep wouldn't come.

Somehow the darkness had suffocating weight tonight.

Noah pressed his palms against dry, blurry eyes then dragged his hands down his cheeks, scraping stubble. He was exhausted yet wide awake. An hour ago, he'd relocated to the couch, hoping for some shuteye.

He was the victim of emotions whipping like trees in a downslope wind.

Why was someone burying a body at an old crime scene?

Why was Val bossing him around like she had the right to?

And why was Kelsie McIlheney here?

Truth be told, his insomnia could be pinned on the woman who'd held his heart in her hand until she'd crushed it.

While he could usually ignore the memories, tonight they were unleashed and roaring.

He'd met Kelsie in middle school. She was born

and raised in Shiloh Peak. He was the new kid whose life had been upended when his father discovered he was doing accounting for a guy who was *not* merely operating fast-food outlets across the country. No, Jack Rollins had been trafficking guns and people, using his restaurants as fronts.

Noah's father had dared to blow the whistle.

When it became clear Rollins was out for lethal revenge, Noah, his parents and his three-year-old brother had been whisked away from Seattle. Gone were his friends and the only life he'd ever known. They'd resettled in a small Appalachian town, and he'd landed in a school a thousand times smaller than the one he'd left behind.

*Traumatized* didn't come close to describing the emotional state of his thirteen-year-old self.

His anger had led to swift and total rebellion. By eighth grade, he'd been well on his way to juvenile detention or worse. At the exact time when he *shouldn't* have been calling attention to his family, he'd been a flashing beacon and proudly so.

He'd managed to get himself expelled from public school. A private school had conditionally accepted him, and his life had changed forever.

He'd met Kelsie McIlheney.

While he'd been a bull crashing through life, she'd been a delicate ballerina.

A literal ballerina.

Kelsie had moved with grace beyond her years.

She'd been absolutely gorgeous, inside and out, light-years out of his league in every way. Even in middle school, she'd received attention for her talent.

She was going places.

He wasn't.

That Thanksgiving, the school took a field trip to see the local girl who was the youngest to dance in the state ballet's Christmas production. He couldn't believe the girl onstage who captivated everyone was the same girl who had left a hefty mark when she took him out of a dodgeball game the week before.

His crush on her had hit him just as hard.

He shifted on the sofa, the images playing like a movie in his mind and making him squishy inside.

They'd been paired up on a history project after Christmas, and the ballerina and the bull became best friends. She'd brought out the best in him. He'd brought out the mischief in her.

Then came junior prom, their first kiss, and the realization there was a lot more to their friendship than either of them had imagined.

When they'd graduated, Kelsie had been headed to the prestigious Ailey School at Fordham University in New York, while Noah had felt the call to law enforcement. Neither had been ready to separate, though they were certain of their callings.

And then everything went wrong.

At the end of the summer, Will Daugherty's parents had gone out of town for a weekend. Will usually threw a bonfire when they left. It was an open secret the Daugherty farm was party central. The gatherings stayed relatively tame, although alcohol flowed freely. Some kids partook, and some didn't.

Will had graduated from the public school a year earlier, but Shiloh Peak was small, and all the kids hung out together. Even graduates from the previous couple years showed up at Will's to join the fun.

Noah and Kelsie had been dating for over a year, and it was to be their final date before she left for New York and he went to the Virginia State Police Academy.

Their future had been murky, but they'd believed they could make it. She was destined for a world-traveling dance troupe. He'd never stand in her way, but he also didn't want to lose what they had. He'd sacrifice his dreams for her if he had to. After all, he could go into law enforcement anywhere.

He'd been running late that night due to his old pickup breaking down on him again. Although he'd tried to notify her, his calls had gone straight to voicemail. His texts had gone unanswered.

Shaking off the memories, Noah stalked to the kitchen. Pulling the fridge open, he stared inside. The cool air doing nothing to soothe the sting of

Kelsie's abrupt departure. She'd been gone when he'd arrived at Will's. Several people said they'd chatted with her. She'd seemed fine, had even dominated in a cornhole tournament.

But no one could remember seeing her after nine. And she'd continued to ignore his calls and texts.

A call to her house let him know her dad had picked her up from Will's and she'd gone straight to bed. When he got up early the next morning to see her off, she was already gone, leaving everything behind for her big-time dreams.

She'd never spoken to him again.

The weird thing was, her "big-time" had never hit. He'd googled Kelsie several times, expecting to find an impressive résumé, but it was like she'd fallen off the face of the earth.

Until today.

Why was she here? And how was he supposed to feel now—

Something scraped near the back door.

Noah stilled. The sound was soft, rhythmic.

He groaned. When he was a kid, a mouse had gnawed his bedroom wall. It had sounded a lot like this.

Back then, that mouse had been one more reason to hate his new hometown. If there had been mice in their Seattle house, those city critters had had the good sense to keep to themselves.

Slamming the refrigerator door, he leaned against it.

Everything in him had wanted to demand answers, but something about Kelsie's demeanor had stopped him. The Kelsie he'd loved had never known fear. Today, she'd reeked of it. It was in the way she jumped when someone approached her blind side. The way she seemed to expect him to pounce.

She was afraid, yet she'd made short work of an attacker with moves worthy of an Olympic-level kickboxer.

So what was going on? How had a rising-star ballerina become a private investigator with the martial arts skills of a crouching tiger?

Given he was the lead on a newly minted homicide investigation that intersected with her old murder investigation, he'd have plenty of chances to find out.

Working with her was going to challenge his heart and mind. He'd loved her. He'd lost her. He'd grieved her. Now she was a stranger he knew way too well.

It was a gut-twisting Twilight Zone.

Wandering into the dark living room, he dropped onto the couch. Dragging his computer onto his lap, he keyed in the password. If he couldn't sleep, he might as well work.

He scrolled through pictures from Burke's Garden, his mushy mind able to do little more than register their existence. Nothing fit into neat boxes. The burial site was difficult to reach, and there were easier places to dispose of remains in the mountains. Why choose a site already on law enforcement's radar?

Was there a serial killer? Had they missed something in the original investigation?

He doubted it. Every shred of evidence pointed to Trenton Daniels murdering Elias Moore. He'd had means, motive, and opportunity. Daniels had lost an inheritance due to Moore's arguments in court. He'd had the murder weapon in his possession and the victim's blood between the hardwood planks in his floor and on clothes buried in the crawlspace. The only thing that hadn't been obvious was whether Daniels had planned the murder or reacted in a crime of passion.

He'd pleaded innocent. The jury had found him guilty. Now he wanted a retrial.

No other bodies had been found at the scene five years earlier, but a team was sweeping the area tonight to be sure. He'd receive their findings in the morning, though he doubted they'd have much to report.

If they found more remains, the defense could raise reasonable doubt by suggesting a serial killer. Reasonable doubt was all—

A dull thud came from the kitchen, as though a bird had flown into a window.

Closing the laptop, Noah listened, his night vision compromised by the screen's light.

The one-story ranch he'd bought a few months

earlier sat in the center of a three-acre wooded lot. Bats were a common sight at night. Maybe one had flown into the window.

Or maybe not. And maybe the earlier scrapes hadn't been a mouse.

Criminals banked on their victims ignoring one out-of-place sound. Maybe he was paranoid, but this didn't feel like something he should ignore.

He was half standing when the back door scraped along the floor.

He turned toward the kitchen, then glanced at the hallway. His bedroom and stored Sig were down the hall. He'd left his phone on the dresser. Should he confront the intruder with his bare hands and no backup? Or should he risk going to the bedroom and turning his back on the person slowly making their way across his kitchen?

He'd take his chances by going for his phone and gun. Without knowing if the person behind the creeping footsteps was armed, he didn't dare go in empty-handed, and he needed to let someone know his home had been invaded.

He padded across the carpet, his thick socks muffling his steps. He rounded the corner to the hallway as the footsteps either stopped or the intruder moved from the tile kitchen to the carpeted living room.

Noah hesitated, but all was silent. Shapes materialized slowly as his eyes readjusted to the darkness. He turned toward his bedroom.

A rustle behind him whipped him around as a hulking shadow tackled him.

Noah landed on his back near the hallway entrance. His head hit the floor. His sinuses rattled as stars shot through his vision.

His attacker loomed over him. The person was bulky, but they moved like a panther, which didn't bode well if he didn't get the upper hand quickly.

Moonlight from the window in his office glinted off something in the intruder's hand. A knife? Something worse? There were only seconds to fight back.

Noah pulled his legs to his chest then kicked, driving his heels into his attacker's knees.

The shadowy figure stumbled, arms flying out. As momentum pitched the person forward, Noah shifted, driving his heels into their stomach.

The figure stumbled backward but stayed upright. Even in the shadows, it was clear they were wearing coveralls and a mask, like the person in Burke's Garden.

The shadow whirled and sprinted away.

Noah sprang to his feet, but the intruder burst out the back door and was deep into the woods by the time Noah reached the back steps.

He couldn't run headlong into the night unarmed. That was the quickest way to die.

Stalking into the house, he flipped on the lights and stepped around glass on the floor. There wasn't time to investigate how the intruder had entered.

He headed for the bedroom, flipping on every light.

Something on the hallway floor stopped his momentum and his heart.

In the office doorway, a syringe lay uncapped, the barrel filled with a liquid that would likely have left him incapacitated...or dead.

# THREE

She should have left town the minute she walked out of the sheriff's department. Should have gone to her car, started the engine, and made her way along the winding mountain roads until she hit 77, then turned toward North Carolina and kept going.

Kelsie's stomach rumbled. She could have hit a drive-through and done something about the gnawing in her stomach, too.

Rolling over on the couch, she picked up her phone to glance at the time. Not quite three thirty.

Tossing her phone, she dropped onto her back and stared at the ceiling, which was illuminated by the light she'd left on in the kitchen. Maybe she should have let Noah bring her dinner.

She might be hungry, but the idea still twisted her gut. Not once since she'd fled Shiloh Peak had she accepted food she didn't either cook or pick up herself. Even in the army, if she didn't open the MRE, she didn't eat it. Her vigilance had had prevented the worst from happening again.

Her stomach complained, and she wrinkled her nose. Vigilance had kept her safe, but it had also made her too hungry to sleep.

Too hungry and too agitated. She'd dropped onto the couch in her clothes, unwilling to go into the bedroom out of sight of the exterior doors.

She usually didn't rattle this way, but being close to the places she used to call home, to the places she used to visit with the people she'd believed she could trust had—

A siren screamed into the night. Another joined in, then another, like a pack of wolves who'd spotted a full moon.

Kelsie leaped up and ran across the living room to the double doors leading to a small balcony. She stepped outside into the frigid night.

Red, white and blue lights spun up as engines roared to life. Below her at the sheriff's department, the parking lot emptied as deputies roared out on an all-hands mission.

Something big had happened to cause a response like this. At this time of night, it was either a massive traffic accident or an officer in trouble.

Whirling, Kelsie stumbled over a canvas chair. Throwing it to the side, heedless of where it landed, she ran into the apartment, grabbed her phone and opened the scanner app. It tended to run on a delay and mostly grabbed dispatch traffic instead of peer-to-peer communications, but it might offer a clue.

She stood in the center of the small living room, staring at the screen. Static cut in and out, but no voices came through.

Kelsie gripped the phone tighter, her heart racing as the static crackled. *Come on*...

A man's voice broke the noise. "Officer needs assistance. Home invasion and assault, 5486 Blue Heron Road." The address bounced in her head, trying to snag a memory. She'd heard it before, but when? Where?

Today...at the sheriff's department... Val had said...

*Noah.*

Noah lived on Blue Heron Road.

Pocketing her phone, Kelsie shoved her feet into her shoes. She tugged on her coat as she ran downstairs, retrieved her pistol from the locked box mounted under the driver's seat in her vehicle, then slid behind the steering wheel with the address already keyed into her phone. She roared out, trailing the deputies' SUVs.

She kept pace with them for the eternity it took to wind around the mountains, her palms sweating and her pulse racing. A response like this meant Noah was either badly injured or law enforcement were starting a manhunt.

Heart pounding, she eased up on the gas and hit the brake as the SUVs in front of her slowed and turned onto a narrow two-lane road. They wound as fast as they dared through the night around twisting turns up a mountain and down the other side. Finally, they hung a left into a driveway that was little more than a two-track dirt path through the woods.

In the clearing in front of a single-story brick house, nearly a dozen vehicles sat, their flashing lights casting eerie dancing shadows in the trees. Law enforcement officials from multiple divisions milled around or headed into the woods with flashlights. One deputy trailed a K-9 around the corner of the house, disappearing into the backyard.

Where was Noah?

There was no ambulance, no paramedics, no indication someone had been injured.

So why was the response so overwhelming?

Killing the engine, Kelsie slipped out of her vehicle and walked toward the house. Maybe no one would notice she was out of place.

Every window blazed with light, and shadows moved past the curtains as though several people milled around inside.

None of this was good.

Although she'd been away from Noah for years and couldn't imagine she'd ever trust him again, her heart needed him to be okay. The idea of living in a world where he wasn't alive and breathing left her brain off-kilter, as though the universe had tilted. He'd once been the person she relied on the most, and although she'd walked away in a haze of fear and pain, he'd often occupied her thoughts. Although she no longer loved him, she needed him to be safe.

There wasn't time to analyze the emotions whipping through her. There were too many physical things to focus on, like keeping up the appearance that she belonged on the scene. While she had her PI credentials, it wasn't likely anyone would let her waltz by them. She kept her head up and moved with purpose toward the front door, her posture daring anyone to stop her.

Confidence could get you farther than—

"Ma'am?" A broad-shouldered highway patrolman stepped into her path. His arched eyebrow was practically a question mark. "Can I help you?"

There were only a few responses that would make it appear she had the right to keep moving. Asking for the sheriff wouldn't work. His name was public. Same with the heads of any other departments. Throwing out Noah's name would raise flags, and this guy was already waving over one of his buddies, clearly suspicious of the stranger in their midst. She only had one other name that might get her through the metaphorical gates. "I'm looking for Special Agent Val Yewell." Noah worked closely with her. If something had happened to him, then she would certainly be on scene.

The trooper—Mason, if she was reading his name tag correctly in the flickering lights—softened, but only slightly. "Name?"

"Kelsie McIlheney." If he was asking, then she'd guessed right about Val. Hopefully, once her name was passed along, Val would give her clearance.

Eyes never leaving her face, Mason relayed her name into the radio on his shoulder. Within seconds, he stepped aside, jerking his chin toward the house. "She's inside. She'll meet you at the front door. Techs are working, so don't enter without her."

"Thank you." Her quaking knees might not make it, but she'd give it all she had. Too many people were on the site and, if crime scene techs were working the scene, something major had happened.

And Val Yewell was inside. Either she was supporting Noah, or she was taking the lead on an investigation into his—

*No.* She wouldn't think the worst.

But what was she walking into? What had happened to bring multiple agencies on the run?

It took a firm grip on the wooden handrail to get up the brick steps to the covered concrete porch.

The scene inside the house was less chaotic than it had appeared from the outside. A deputy stood at the head of a hallway to the left, while two crime scene techs worked the area behind him. A plainclothes officer slowly worked his way around the living room, searching the carpet and furniture with precision.

There was, thankfully, no blood.

From the right, out of sight around a corner, indistinct voices drifted to her.

There were no gurneys, no coroners, no indication anyone was hurt or dead.

Relief drained her strength. She'd grip the door frame for support if she wasn't trained to preserve evidence.

The officer spotted her, took her info, then disappeared around the corner toward the voices, leaving her alone in the doorway.

She looked around the living room. If the situation wasn't so dire, she'd smile. Noah had never been one for frills. The house was practical, but it wasn't what she'd call homey. The den held a couch, where Noah's laptop sat. A large TV mounted over the fireplace dominated the room, while two mismatched chairs sat wherever they'd seemed to fit. Two end tables each held a different lamp, and there was a coffee table with papers and files scattered across the wood. Not a single piece of furniture matched.

Yep. That was on brand for the man she'd known.

Val Yewell stepped around the corner, her expression tight. She narrowed her eyes, but there was more curiosity than concern in her expression. "The porch has been cleared. Wait out there." She turned and walked back around the corner.

Okay, then. Either she had really bad news, or she wanted Kelsie away from the crime scene.

Anxiety crept in, tensing her muscles until pain pulsed with every heartbeat. Walking to the railing, Kelsie wrapped her fingers around the painted wood and stared at her SUV parked beside the driveway. If she believed in prayer, now would be a good time to speak.

But God couldn't be trusted to answer, and she had nothing to say to Him anyway.

"Why are you here?" The voice behind her was deeper than she'd prepared for.

Her fingers flexed. A splinter punctuated the question with pain she barely registered. *If* she had prayed, and *if* she believed God answered prayers, she'd offer him a big, relieved *thank you*.

Turning, she leaned against the railing and crossed her arms over her chest to keep her spine from dropping her in a heap to the concrete.

Noah stood in the doorway, his face a mask of oddly shifting shadows in the flashing emergency lights. It was impossible to read his expression, but his posture was ramrod straight. "I asked a question."

Yes, he had. Now that she was facing him, the only answer she could give made her sound like an ambulance-chasing thrill-seeker...or a stalker.

Kelsie cleared her throat and pulled her confidence mask out of her hip pocket. Telling the truth with authority might make it land more like she was a professional investigator than a stalker. "I heard the sirens, pulled up my scanner app, recognized your address and thought I'd make sure everything was okay." Simple. To the point. No apologies.

"I'm fine."

She winced as the edge in his voice sliced her. He'd been friendly earlier, but she'd wounded him by not accepting his offer of help for dinner. "What happened?"

With spare details, he unwound an account about fighting an intruder in his house.

An intruder who wore the same coveralls as her opponent in the woods.

She should have fought harder. She should have pursued her assailant. She should have prevailed. If she had, then Noah wouldn't have had to fight alone the way she'd had to fight for sixteen years.

This was all her fault.

The realization twisted her gut and caught in her throat. She'd let the suspect get away, and—

"Noah." Val appeared behind Noah, holding her phone, her expression grim. "We need to talk." Her gaze shifted to Kelsie. "And you, come inside. This affects you, too."

"You're sure?" There was no way he was hearing Val correctly. Noah stared at the back door, trying to process everything. Someone had duct-taped the windowpane closest to the lock to hold the glass together, used a blunt object to break it without shattering it, then reached inside to unlock the door.

It was all so simple.

He was buying an alarm system and a windowless door as soon as was humanly possible.

Forcing his whipping attention back to Val, he did his best to ignore Kelsie, who stood beside him radiating either arrogance or discomfort.

"I'm waiting for photos and a more detailed report." Val glanced at her phone. "But there's no reason for our techs to lie." The wry sarcasm in the statement was familiar but unwarranted. All of them were exhausted, and she'd doled out some pretty shocking discoveries from the Burke's Garden scene. Now wasn't the time to be flippant.

Kelsie turned away, staring out the window over the sink. "I need to call my boss." She didn't reach for her phone. Instead she eyed the darkness on the other side of the glass as though she wished she could disappear into it.

Like the guy who'd tried to shoot him up with an as-yet-undetermined substance to either incapacitate or kill him. Lab results would tell the tale.

At this point, with his adrenaline ebbing and his thoughts whiplashing, Noah wasn't sure what was more shocking…the assault, Kelsie's presence, or the three other sets of remains the techs had discovered in Burke's Garden.

Buried remains were always a *terrible* discovery. Three more bodies were a *horrifying* discovery. Those three plus the one Kelsie's attacker had left behind indicated a possible serial killer.

A possible serial killer meant Trenton Daniels might be an innocent man. At the very least, the discovery of more bodies in the same spot where they'd found Elias Moore would cast reasonable doubt on his guilt.

Noah dragged his hand down his face. If the remains had been out there longer than five years, then the state had missed something huge during the original investigation. If it had been less than five years, then the defense could argue a serial killer had murdered Elias Moore and had continued to kill while Daniels sat in prison. "How long before we get preliminary times of death?"

"Not long. The coroner is working on it." Val's sarcasm had vanished. She looked as exhausted as he felt. "This doesn't mean we missed something with Daniels. If the method is different, then we may be dealing with two different killers."

"Using the same burial ground?" Kelsie turned toward them. She held up a hand as though she knew Noah was about to argue. "Before you get defensive, my team is not out to poke holes in the initial investigation or to make accusations. Trinity sent me to make sure the prosecution's case is airtight, that there are no legs for this retrial to stand on. We're here to protect you."

Maybe, but it still felt like the state didn't trust them.

Val rubbed her temple with two fingers. "Four more bodies is a lot of reasonable doubt."

"Under the right circumstances, yes, but I have bigger questions." Kelsie adjusted her ponytail then met Noah's eyes for one of the first times since he'd run into her a few hours earlier. "Why did someone break in your house tonight? Someone dressed exactly like the suspect in Burke's Garden? Is it because you got a good look at them today? Or is this about something different?"

Val tipped her head in an exaggerated motion that tossed a silent *good question* into the mix.

It *was* a good question, but there were no good answers.

"If this was about witnessing them at the crime scene today—" Val lowered her hand from her temple "—then why weren't you a target, Ms. McIlheney?"

Kelsie rocked backward as though Val had slapped her, but she quickly reset her expression. "I don't—"

"Special Agent Cross?" They all turned toward the voice from the living room. One of their crime scene techs, a new guy Noah had never met before, motioned for him to speak in private.

With a quick glance at Val, Noah started to step around Kelsie but stopped mere inches from her, the closest he'd been to her in years. "Call your boss. Find out how he wants you to proceed." He swallowed his pride and his personal questions. There was more at stake here than the scars on his wounded heart. "I'm willing to get you authorization to work with us on this if the state will sign off on it." If Daniels was innocent, he needed to be cleared. If he wasn't, then they needed to make sure he wasn't released on a technicality and that they apprehended the new killer who was hiding behind door number two.

He didn't wait for Kelsie to respond. Instead, he slipped past her and walked into the den.

It was funny how his house looked exactly the same as it had an hour earlier, yet the air felt horribly different. He'd worked breaking-and-enterings, armed robberies, assaults, murders...but he'd never been on the receiving end. All of those times he's thought he was being compassionate, he hadn't had a clue how the victims were feeling. His house felt dirty, as though it needed to be bleached from top to bottom. The walls had eyes, and he was pretty sure he would jump at every sound for the next month. After all, ignoring what his ears had warned him to pay attention to had nearly gotten him killed.

He shook off the sensations crawling across his skin and tried to shift into his role as investigator, but with the crime scene in his own living room, it was a tough ask. "What did you find?"

The new guy glanced around as though he wanted to be certain no one was listening. He was young, probably midtwenties. He might even be fresh out of college. He seemed to have experience because he was calm and professional, unlike some of the new hires, who could be a little too eager to be of help at their first few crime scenes.

Maybe he'd already worked a murder or two. That sobered up even the most enthusiastic new hires quickly.

When the tech seemed to be satisfied no one was in earshot, he turned his attention to Noah. "I wasn't sure how much you'd want the PI to know, so I called you over."

*Smart.* Private investigators weren't often read in on every little detail. They operated on a need-to-know basis, and sometimes what they needed to know was nothing. He'd be as open with Kelsie as the state required him to be, but until then, he'd hold a few things close to the vest. "What did you find?" It almost made him shudder to ask while he was standing in front of his own coffee table.

"We ran a presumptive field test on the syringe."

Noah's heart thunked painfully against his ribs. He was about to have at least one answer. Did he want it? "And?"

"Flunitrazepam."

This guy was definitely new if he was throwing around technical names.

The street names scraped Noah's raw nerves. *Rohypnol. Roofies.* "So someone wanted to incapacitate me?" *But why?*

"No, sir. That syringe was loaded." The tech shook his head, his expression darkening. "Special Agent Cross, the amount in that syringe could have killed you."

# FOUR

The sky was fading from deep black to navy blue when Kelsie shifted her SUV into Park by the door to her temporary apartment. Exhaustion weighed down every limb as though they were bound to twenty-pound dumbbells.

If she'd felt safe, she'd forget about dragging herself up the stairs. She'd lay her head on the steering wheel and sleep until she couldn't sleep anymore.

In the sheriff's department's adjoining lot, several deputies pulled in and exited their vehicles, gathering in the space near the building to talk with somber expressions.

If she knew them, she'd join them and see what they thought about what had happened at Noah's.

As it was, she had no clue. He'd talked for a long time to the crime scene tech, then he'd called Val into the conversation, leaving Kelsie alone in the kitchen. She'd tried to eavesdrop, but they'd disappeared up the hallway, and the distance had muffled their voices.

Whatever they'd discovered, they wanted to keep the interloper out of it.

If she'd had more energy, she'd be furious. As it was, she'd have to sleep before she could even think about working herself into outrage.

Or maybe not. An ember burned in her belly. Noah had said he'd work with her, would keep her in the loop. Five seconds later, he'd shut her out.

The ember quickly flamed out, leaving only bitter smoke behind. Guess he didn't trust her any more than she trusted him.

She had reason to be wary. What were his motives?

It was too much to think about when her brain was mush and her body was shutting down from hunger and exhaustion.

Leaning forward, she looked for the deputies and found them right where she'd last seen them, still talking, still in range to help if she were to need someone.

While there was some question about the attacker's motive at Noah's house, she felt like he was the target more than she was. If this was really about them seeing the killer at Burke's Garden, then the easier prey was Kelsie, the newcomer who was in an unfamiliar apartment near the crime scene. Taking the trouble to figure out who Noah was and where he lived felt very personal.

Or she could be wrong.

She eyed the deputies again. They hadn't moved.

Normally, she wasn't so squirrelly about her safety. The army had trained her well. Her coaches had trained her well. Her fellow Trinity investigator, Rebecca Campbell, liked to call her a "deceptively graceful lethal weapon." Everyone knew she could take care of herself.

But now? Everything was off-kilter, and she was so tired she couldn't stave off the memories that had driven her from these mountains years earlier. Even her parents had left, moving to Delaware when her father retired.

She felt trapped. She couldn't leave, even though she desperately wanted to flee the broken images from her past. There was no way Elliott would send in a pinch hitter, not without asking questions she didn't want to answer. She didn't want to explain things she'd never spoken out loud, things that still sometimes dragged her out of sleep, paralyzed and sweating.

She shoved open the door and let the truth slip around the brick walls she'd built around her heart. Someone had attacked Noah, and she couldn't leave this place and its horrible memories until she knew that person had been put behind bars. Noah had to be safe.

Once upon a time, he'd been her best friend and later her first love. Despite her pain, a deep-seated loyalty demanded she protect him, though she would keep herself emotionally distant.

Now that she'd looked him in the eye, keeping her distance might be more difficult than she'd anticipated.

She'd blown it yesterday by not taking down her attacker. Kelsie opened the back door and grabbed her backpack, pulling it from the rear of the vehicle with a little too much force. Her failure had nearly gotten Noah killed. If she'd have been less focused on her own trauma and more focused on her surroundings, then the killer wouldn't have surprised her. If a thousand things had been different, then Noah would have never been in danger.

She had to do better. She had to defeat the monsters.

The SUV rocked when she slammed the door.

"I'm pretty sure your car doesn't deserve that abuse."

Kelsie flung her backpack to the ground and whirled toward the voice, fists in striking position.

Several feet away, Val Yewell held up her hands and took a step back. "It's just me." She lowered her arms slowly. "I'm impressed with your reaction time, though."

"What do you want?" Kelsie was too tired for this woman's games. She snatched her bag off the ground and rested her hand on the driver's door. Should she take her gun or leave it securely stowed?

It wasn't like she needed it. She'd spent fifteen

years studying Muay Thai and was an expert in the martial art. She'd never wanted to be caught with no way to defend herself again.

"I was wondering if we could talk." Val shoved her hands into the pockets of her dark gray slacks. Her eyes were heavy with shadows. The night had been long and exhausting for all of them, though for entirely different reasons.

Hoisting her backpack onto one shoulder, Kelsie eyed Noah's partner. The woman was nosy, like most investigators tended to be.

There was something else though. The way she looked at Kelsie was too knowing. It was as though she could read her thoughts and knew her entire history.

No one, not even the one or two people she considered friends, knew the truth about her past.

No one ever would.

Kelsie shook her head. "Not now. I'd like to sleep for a few hours before today kicks in with more fun." Her body was too tired to be hungry, but it wouldn't be long before her stomach sounded an alarm, and she'd like to get a solid nap first.

At least, that was what she'd tell Val if the other woman tried to push her into a discussion.

"I get that." Val turned to walk away then stopped and looked back. Something in her posture was different, softer, as though she'd shed her professional demeanor. "Look, I…" She scanned the ever-lightening sky. "I went into law enforcement for a reason, and I feel like you did, too." Taking a deep breath, she turned to stare at the deputies who were still knotted together on the far side of the parking lot. "It's not easy to talk about, but talking about it takes away its power."

Kelsie's stomach dropped. She tightened her grip on her backpack's strap. What did Val know?

"Anyway, I hope you get some rest." Without looking back, Val disappeared around Kelsie's vehicle.

Shame and fear and the urge to be heard went to war, surging white-hot energy through Kelsie's veins.

She fled. Punching in the code to unlock the exterior door, she raced up the stairs then slammed the door to the apartment and locked it behind her.

The lights still blazed from the night before.

What would her team at Trinity think if they saw her, Kelsie the Strong, Kelsie the Brave, Kelsie the Powerful, as she cowered against the door? What would they think if they witnessed her looking under both beds, in both closets and in the bathtub for anyone who could sneak up on her, before she stopped in the middle of the small apartment and stared at the door, shaking from exhaustion and adrenaline?

She'd joined the army years ago not just to escape, but to prove to herself she could never be defeated again. She'd learned to defend herself. She'd supported others in dangerous situations.

Now here she was, within minutes of her old hometown, of her old home memories, afraid of the dark, afraid of the shadows...

And afraid of the truth.

Hopefully, Kelsie had gotten more sleep than he had.

Noah leaned against the wall outside of her apartment and stared at the sheriff's department across the parking lot. Last night's response had been swift and strong. He'd thought it overdone at first, until he'd learned about the additional bodies found in Burke's Garden.

Law enforcement suspected a serial killer hunting in the area. When an agent involved in the discovery was attacked in his house, it had sent the cavalry running, hunting, searching.

He'd collapsed across his bed into a restless sleep as the sun came up, while a handful of deputies and field agents searched the woods on his property.

They'd come up empty-handed. Whoever had tried to load him up with Rohypnol had disappeared, leaving behind only a few broken branches and some indistinct footprints.

Shivering against the midmorning chill, Noah sipped the coffee he'd brought from home. While the promised snow from the day before had held off, the cloudy skies above declared winter didn't need snow to bring on a deep freeze.

Maybe he should have brought coffee for Kelsie, but after she'd bluntly turned down his offer to bring her food when she was clearly starving, he wasn't inclined to try again. Something in her demeanor said she didn't trust him.

That was a sharp, stinging cut. There was a time when the only people either of them had trusted had been one another. Clearly, something had nuked that in a way he'd never seen coming.

He wished he knew what he'd done.

At the sound of footfalls on the stairs, he straightened and moved away from the door. As jumpy as Kelsie was, he didn't want to startle her, although she should be expecting him. He'd texted her an hour earlier to see if she wanted to go to Bramwell to look into a lead. He'd talked to his counterparts in West Virginia and had cleared the way to speak to a few people without stepping on anyone in WVA law enforcement's toes.

She opened the door, stepped into the cold midmorning and looked straight at him, as though she'd calculated exactly where he'd be standing.

How did she manage to look like she'd slept a full eight hours? Her ponytail was as perfect as ever, and she moved like the classical ballet dancer she'd once trained to be. She was all beauty and poise and grace.

Meanwhile, he felt and looked like a freight

train had dragged him for a couple of miles over broken rail ties during a blizzard.

Noah focused on Kelsie's large to-go cup from Brewed Awakening. The family-owned place was across the street from her apartment and served coffee that was legendary in the area. "I see you've already been out and about."

It seemed to take her a second to process his words. Likely, they weren't what she'd been expecting. "Twice. Turns out they make a pretty good breakfast sandwich, and one cup of coffee wasn't enough."

So she really *was* as tired as he was. She was just better at hiding it. Had she slept at all? Or was she running on caffeine and adrenaline, the same way he hoped to make it through the day?

He pulled his keys from his pocket and pointed to his SUV parked near the street. "We'll head to—"

"I'm right here." Kelsie stepped toward her blue SUV, parked close to the door. "I'll drive. I remember how to get to Bramwell." She was inside the vehicle before he could muster an argument.

And boy, did he want to argue. He was assigned to this case. She was here by invitation. She didn't get to control anything, including the drive to—

An old memory stirred, and he walked around to the passenger door. Pulling it open, he looked across the front seat at her. "You still get carsick, don't you?" She'd been legendary back in the day.

Having Kelsie as a passenger meant being prepared to pull over at a moment's notice. It had always been easier to let her drive, and there had been countless times when he'd simply handed her the keys to his old pickup rather than deal with whatever came next. They'd spent a lot of hours winding around the mountains with the windows down, singing at the top of their lungs to the radio, filling in the blank spots with loud voices when the signal faded in the valleys.

The quick flash of the past tugged something in his heart, but he ignored it as he slid into the SUV and shut the door. Those days were long gone.

Kelsie pushed the button to start the vehicle. "Yeah. Sure." She glanced at the rear camera, then looked over her shoulder as she backed out, navigating the narrow parking lot. "How is Special Agent Whitmire?"

He'd spoken to her husband on the drive over. "Mom and baby are both doing great." He'd have to send a gift or flowers or something. The jury was out, though, on whether he was glad her daughter's early arrival had shoved him back into Kelsie's life.

Buckling his seat belt, Noah settled in for the ride to Bramwell, about an hour away. He hadn't missed that Kelsie had been weird about his carsick question, but he'd let it go for now. Maybe all those years of car sickness had created a need for control. Maybe her need to be behind the wheel was something more. He had no idea what made her act so squirrelly.

The light floral scent of her shampoo drifted to him, the same she'd always used, and the memories floated on the air as well. No matter how much he wanted to pretend she was a stranger, his head and heart remembered her. It was like an out-of-body experience to be around her, this person who used to know him so well, this person he'd known better than he knew himself.

That person was a stranger now. It was like living in some sort of science-fiction parallel universe.

"So." Kelsie broke the silence and drew him away from memories of rambling mountain drives. "Your text said you got details about one of the victims found last night. Care to share?"

*Oh yeah. The case.* He needed to focus on that and not on the woman beside him. "The coroner got an ID on the remains in the process of being buried." He pulled the email up and opened the attachment. "Jaxon Collins. Male. Age thirty-four. Got a list of priors that takes up a couple of pages, mostly drug-related. Last known address is in Bramwell, and last known place of employment is the soda shop." He watched Kelsie as he delivered the information.

Her fingers tightened around the steering wheel. While they'd grown up and gone to school in Shiloh Peak, the surrounding small towns had been their stomping grounds. Bramwell's corner soda shop had been one of their favorite places to visit when they'd taken their rambling, noisy drives through the mountains.

He'd given her a heads-up on the town to give her time to process, but he'd wanted to toss out the actual location on the fly so he could witness her reaction.

His gut had been right. Something about being back in the area was eating at her. But was it him? Or was it something else?

She seemed to school her expression, though her knuckles on the steering wheel gave away her tension. After a measured inhale, she cleared her throat. "What about next of kin?"

"That's not a fun answer. His mother passed away when he was fourteen. His dad's response upon notification of his son's murder was, 'Haven't seen the deadbeat in years, and I ain't sorry.'" What happened in families to cause such deep division? He'd seen it many times over the years and, had he made different choices when he was rebelling in middle school, he might have gone down the same path.

He might have…had it not been for the woman beside him.

"Ouch." Kelsie winced and eased her grip on the steering wheel. "I hate stories like that, but sometimes I understand…" She trailed off, then came back stronger. "Did Jaxon Collins have a roommate?"

*Hang on.* They needed to circle back to her unfinished sentence. What did she understand? Her mother had always pushed her to be a dancer in a way Kelsie had resented. Had she broken ties with her parents? Was that why she'd disappeared? Why they'd eventually left the area? Then why had she cut him out of—

"Noah. Roommate?"

*Fine.* Let her be evasive. For now. Eventually, they were going to have the conversation his heart was begging for. He deserved answers.

"The property address is likely a dead end." He glanced at the phone again. "Tax records indicate it's owned by a guy who seems to have no connection to him."

"He probably picked a random address so he'd have something to put down on his tax forms."

That was the most likely scenario. Plenty of addicts he'd interacted with over the years banked on their employers simply being satisfied to have something on record. "Merely checking boxes works in favor of someone who wants to hide. It's not too hard to cover your tracks if you don't want to be found."

The air in the car seemed to thicken.

He hadn't meant to hint at her disappearing act, but there it was, out in the open as though he'd intended to lob a spear right at her.

Maybe he had.

"People have a lot of reasons for not wanting to be found." Her voice was tight, and she let her words hang before she spoke again. "It's also possible Collins was simply without a place to live and picked an address in town because he read the number on the mailbox." The words fell flat.

She wasn't taking the bait, intended or not.

They were silent the rest of the way to Bramwell. The farther they went along the road that twisted along the river, the more Kelsie tensed. Her shoulders stiffened, and her grip on the steering wheel tightened. If she kept this up, her skeleton would pop out of her skin.

There was nothing he could say to relax her, not when he had no idea what was causing her stress. Clearly, whatever trust they'd shared in the past was long gone, because she offered him no explanations.

Kelsie pulled into a gravel lot across from the visitors' center and pressed the button to shut off the engine. For long, silent moments, she stared out the front window toward the old railway cars by the museum, which told the story of the town's glory days, back when the owners of the nearby coal mines had built their mansions along "Millionaires' Row."

Maybe she was about to start talking. Maybe she was about to offer an olive branch. Maybe—

"See that Jeep?" Her head turned, her gaze following a gray four-door Jeep Wrangler towing an ATV as it slowed at the slight bend in the road before cruising by them along the small Main Street.

"Yeah?" He watched as it disappeared around the corner. "There are a ton of them around." Four-wheel drives were plentiful in the area, and Wranglers in particular were a dime a dozen.

Kelsie glanced at him as she opened her car door. "It might be a coincidence, but I changed lanes and speeds a few times, and I'm pretty sure he was following us."

# FIVE

Noah stared up the street, past the old stone church, watching to see if the Jeep reappeared.

A couple of all-terrain vehicles roared by, headed for the popular Hatfield-McCoy Trail System that ran through the area, but nothing else moved.

Despite the intrusion at his house, he was more worried about Kelsie's safety than his own. There was no proof he was the sole target.

Worse, Kelsie seemed antsy, maybe even paranoid. Something had happened that had changed her. As much as he was angry with her for leaving him without an explanation, he was also concerned.

The tug-of-war was real.

And the town of Bramwell wasn't helping.

Walking up the sidewalk with the brick buildings of Main Street to their left and the old Millionaires' Row houses on their right made time fold onto itself. They'd come here often back in the day, racing into the soda shop for a good burger and the best chili cheese fries on the planet. If he closed his eyes, he might be that carefree high schooler again, his only concern being he hadn't studied for Mr. Gage's algebra final.

That and how he and Kelsie were going to hold it together after graduation when she was in New York and he was here.

How was she here today, the same and yet so different? The woman he knew so well and yet a stranger?

Noah forced his fingers to remain straight instead of balling into a fist. This was a job, not a trip down a memory lane that a rockslide had destroyed. He should be focused, watching the area for threats, not wrestling with the pain he'd endured at the hands of the woman walking beside him.

He cleared his throat. "What makes you think we were followed?"

She walked with purpose, her gaze straight ahead and her shoulders squared. "I'm not certain. I mean, it could be coincidence. This place reinvented itself from coal mining kingdom to all-terrain vehicle playground, so maybe... Maybe they were headed this way and fell in behind us."

She wasn't wrong. While the winter months were often snow-covered and cold, the Hatfield-McCoy Trail System drew ATV enthusiasts from all over. Those trails kept these small towns alive.

It was possible the Jeep belonged to an outdoorsman who'd happened to be going their way.

It was also possible it didn't.

Kelsie scanned the area. "I didn't get a plate number, did you?"

"No." Noah kept pace beside her, although he held his distance on the narrow sidewalk. That was something he'd never done in the past. If they weren't holding hands, they'd bumped elbows or shoulders and not thought twice. "Right now, we're knee-deep in so many things it's easy to see a bad guy behind every bush." He stepped up to open the door to the soda shop, then ushered her in ahead of him.

Stepping into the warmth of the eclectic diner was like stepping out of a time machine. It was darker inside than outside, but it was still cheery and nostalgic. A long counter ran to the left, part soda fountain, part ice-cream freezer. A blend of fifties memorabilia and ATV posters cluttered bookcases and shelves along the walls. Several tables lined the narrow dining area. While the front room was vacant, voices came from a door to the left that led to a larger main dining area. Sixties music bounced in from a hidden speaker.

Memories rushed back with the scent of burgers and fries blended with something sweet and wonderful.

Noah wanted to close his eyes, to allow long-buried memories to have their moment in the sun.

From birthday parties to group hangouts to simple lunches, Kelsie was in nearly every memory he had of this place. The rush of emotion was as warm and sweet as hot fudge on one of their famous sundaes. For a moment, he wished he could forget what had happened between them and start over.

He shook off the longing. Like too much sugar could make him sick, too much trust in a woman who'd kicked him in the teeth could ruin him. It was best to keep the status quo.

Even if it hurt.

Kelsie trailed Noah to the counter, where they waited a few seconds before a man stepped in from the door to the main dining room. He was a few years older than them, tall and thin. He had floppy dark hair threaded with streaks of gray and kind brown eyes that lit when he spotted Noah. "Hey, man! Haven't seen you in a couple of months." He flicked a glance at Kelsie, but his expression revealed no recognition. "You want a table?"

"Not today, Sean." Noah's voice was low and heavy with the gravity of their mission. Sean was a friend, and he hated to drag him into this mess. "I'm actually here on business."

Sean straightened and rested his hands on the counter, his gaze bouncing from Noah to Kelsie. "What's wrong? Are my people okay?"

"Your people?" Kelsie seemed confused by the phrase.

To be honest, it did sound a little mafia-like. Knowing the way Sean treated his staff, though, it was a family dynamic and nothing sinister.

Sean must have noticed Kelsie's tone, because he directed his next words to her. "We have a lot of high school kids who work here, and it'd kill me if—" He looked back to Noah. "They're all okay?"

"The kids are fine." Noah tapped on his phone and held up a photo of Jaxon Collins.

He didn't offer a name or any identifying information. It was best to see if Collins had represented himself to Sean as someone different, maybe using an alias or offering up more about his identity than they'd uncovered.

"What did he do now?" Sean waved the photo away with a dismissive exhale.

"Now?" *Interesting.* Opening the Notes app on his phone, Noah arched an eyebrow. "So he's not been the best employee?"

"Not really. We hired him a few months ago, probably around the last time you were in here. He was a friend of one of my cooks, Braden. We knew he had a history, but we hired him to do prep work because he swore he was clean. He was hit-and-miss about showing up, but the owners wanted to give him a chance. Last time I saw him was a week ago, maybe? He's missed all of his shifts since. I gave up on him, figured he'd backslid into a bad place."

"Is Braden here?" That seemed like their best bet for finding out more. He scanned the familiar room.

Through an open pass-through, the kitchen was visible. Several young men and women were working with one eye on their tasks and one on the conversation.

Two waitresses, a blonde and a brunette, walked out of the door to the other dining room, laughing. They sobered quickly, their steps stuttering, when they spotted Noah and Kelsie, but they kept moving.

"Tracey." At Sean's call, the brunette stopped and looked over her shoulder. "When you go into the kitchen, can you send Braden out?"

"Sure." The woman, in her midtwenties, didn't hide her curious look, but she was quick to deliver the request to one of the cooks near the back of the room.

He looked up through the pass-through before heading out. He, too, was in his midtwenties. He was about six feet, muscular, and wearing a backward baseball cap over thick brown hair. "You guys need something?" He looked at Sean. "There a problem with the food?"

"No." Sean tipped his head toward Noah. "You've probably seen Noah here before, although it's been a couple of months."

"You're vaguely familiar, sure." Braden's eyebrows knit in confusion.

Noah almost felt sorry for him. They needed to move the questioning along and get this guy out of the misery of thinking he'd done his job poorly. He held up his credentials. "Braden, I'm Special Agent Noah Cross. I work for the Bureau of Investigation in Virginia." Pocketing his ID, he held up the phone. "What can you tell me about this man?"

"Jaxon?" Braden visibly paled, and his voice went up a notch. "What about him?"

"When's the last time you saw him?"

"Maybe a week or so ago? We leave our ATVs parked here and hit the trails after work most days. He went with us, but it's been a few days ago." Braden seemed nervous. His gaze flitted among them. "Did he do something wrong? I vouched for him to work here." He turned toward Sean. "If he did anything, I'm sorry."

Sean rested a hand on Braden's shoulder, but he focused on Noah. "What's this about? You're looking for something, and I understand, but can you give us an idea of what's happened?"

Behind him, Kelsie tensed. He could hear the hitch in her breathing. Was she struggling with their shared memories as much as he was?

That wasn't important now. Forcing himself to the task at hand, Noah glanced at his phone, pocketed it and waited a beat, wishing he didn't have to deliver bad news. "Jaxon Collins was found dead yesterday." The less details he offered, the more authentic reactions he was likely to get.

"Oh man." Sean pulled his hand from Braden's shoulder and dragged it through his hair. "I knew he wasn't doing the greatest, but I didn't think... Well, I didn't *want* to think..."

Braden's chin dropped to his chest. "Did he OD?"

"We're unsure of his cause of death at this point." Noah held the truth close to the vest. "We were hoping you could offer us some insight."

"I've got nothing, but you can talk with the rest of the staff one-on-one if you need to." Sean was pale and shaken.

Braden answered a few more questions, obviously shocked by the news of Jaxon's death. He didn't have much to offer, and he returned to the kitchen quietly, clearly rattled by what he'd learned.

Noah spent the next few minutes talking to the rest of the staff. Few of them knew Jaxon well, and most simply mentioned only seeing him a time or two given his hit-and-miss work ethic.

By the time they'd finished their brief interviews and stepped out onto the sidewalk, they were no closer to answers than they had been when they'd started out.

Noah stared up the street, discouraged. "I was hoping for some angle, some lead. This was a bust." It had been a colossal waste of time in addition to ripping open his heart so the memories poured out. He was drawn to Kelsie, even though he knew she was nothing but pain.

"Well, we still have his address, so we—"

"Special Agent Cross?" The blonde waitress, Priscilla something, slipped out the door and eased it shut as though she was afraid she might get caught talking to him. She stepped closer, wringing her hands and looking up the street from left to right. Her gaze landed on Kelsie, though she seemed confused. "Can we talk?"

Whatever was going on, it was clear Priscilla was more comfortable talking to a woman.

No problem.

Noah stepped to the side, and Kelsie moved to stand closer to Priscilla.

The young woman was silent, winding her fingers together in an anxious twist.

They'd talked to her earlier, and she'd been antsy, but that could have been from the common fear of answering questions from a law enforcement officer. Sometimes, it was tough to tell what was guilt and what was fear.

Kelsie tilted her head down toward the young woman. "Priscilla, did you remember something?"

"No. There was something I couldn't say in there." Priscilla looked over her shoulder at the door, then back at Kelsie. "I know what might have happened to Jaxon."

\* \* \*

Kelsie wrestled to hold herself together. Priscilla had information, and her attention needed to focus on that.

But the past wouldn't let go. Everything beneath Kelsie's skin felt like she was on a perpetual roller coaster, diving and looping. If she made it out of Bramwell without losing the two cups of coffee and the breakfast sandwich from Brewed Awakening, then she might start praying again.

Clearly, being close to home was twisting her mind in more ways than she could count if prayer was on her mind. If God was going to let bad things happen to her, then she didn't need to be talking to Him.

Did she?

"Priscilla?" Noah's voice was gentle, nudging Kelsie's thoughts onto a smoother path. "It's safe to talk to us."

The fear in Priscilla Lambert's eyes erased Kelsie's anxiety. This girl was struggling with something, and she needed help.

Kelsie stepped closer to the young woman. The presence of law enforcement seemed to be triggering Priscilla. "Would you like to talk in private?"

Priscilla shook her head. "No. I told them I remembered something Jaxon said the last night he worked, but there's more. I don't want someone to overhear me."

Behind Kelsie, Noah tensed, but she managed

to keep the increased beat of her heart from breaking into her expression. "You talk. We'll listen."

Drawing a shaky breath, Priscilla kneaded her clasped fingers. "I was dating Jaxon." She lowered her voice. "Management doesn't like employees dating. It's tough if there's a breakup. Drama's nasty, ya know?"

Kelsie fought to keep from clenching her fists in frustration. Two consenting adults dating wasn't a crime. She tried to steer the conversation to relevant details. "How long did you date?"

"A couple of weeks. Like, we went out a few times, but listen... Jaxon wasn't using. He used to, but he'd stopped."

Doubtful. It wouldn't be the first time an addict had lied or made promises he couldn't keep.

There was no sense in hurting the young woman by saying that. "So what do you think happened?"

"I don't know. Jaxon was clean, but he was... twitchy. When we went out, it was in Bluefield or Shiloh Peak, to the movies or to grab something to eat. But he was always looking over his shoulder. One time, we went for ice cream up on Walker Mountain. A bunch of guys came in the store. I didn't get a good look at them, but Jaxon got all sweaty and we left without ice cream. He said he started feeling bad."

What had Jaxon been mixed up in? Were they dealing with organized crime? Gang violence?

"Would you recognize the men if you saw them again?"

"Like I said, I didn't pay attention. I saw a big group then we were out of there." Priscilla chewed her bottom lip. "Maybe it wasn't even a thing?"

"Possibly." Noah spoke over Kelsie's shoulder. "But we need to follow every lead. Do you remember a day and time? We can check cameras, look for witnesses."

With an apologetic wince, Priscilla shook her head. "I don't. Maybe a month ago? It was a weekday, I think." She exhaled, looking sheepish. "Since I started working here about two months ago, my days all mush together because my weekends aren't weekends anymore."

"I understand." Noah reached into his pocket and passed her a business card. "You can call me if you remember anything else."

"Thanks." Priscilla pocketed the card and turned to go inside, then hesitated. "You won't tell anyone we were dating, will you?"

"Not unless it's necessary." Noah offered a thin smile.

He couldn't make any promises when their investigation was active.

"Thanks." Priscilla slipped back inside, looking slightly relieved.

The street was quiet, though a couple of ATV engines revved in the distance, closer to the trails.

Noah waited for the door to close then pointed

up the street toward the old stone church. "The house where Jaxon claimed to live is that way."

They were across the street before Kelsie felt free to speak. "What do you think about Priscilla?" The girl was scared, though there could have been any number of reasons.

"My honest opinion?"

"No, I want you to lie to me." It popped out of her mouth before she could stop it, an old comeback she hadn't said to anyone in years. In this moment with Noah, it was natural.

Kelsie smiled for the first time since she'd crossed the state line into Virginia. Something about the exchange felt right. Or maybe assuaging Priscilla's fears had taken the focus off her own. Either way, she felt a little less like her skeleton was going to crawl out of her skin. She felt somewhat…normal.

Whatever *normal* was.

Noah smiled. It was a genuine grin, one she recognized from years ago.

He had the kind of smile that went all the way to his eyes and transformed his face into something delicious and irresistible. The kind of smile that could make a girl forget her fears.

Maybe she should.

Boy, did she want to.

But the fears were bigger than she was. Bigger than both of them. They'd become entrenched over half of a lifetime, and they wouldn't uproot easily. They craved darkness, and her mind and heart were filled with shadows in which to hide from Noah's light.

"Okay." Noah was oblivious to the battle raging inside of her. "My honest thought is nothing is going to help us unless we get more details. I mean, we'll look into it, but—"

"But people who *are* using or who *have been* using run into old dealers all the time, and sometimes they still owe those dealers a lot of money."

"Exactly. While it's possible we've got a dealer taking out his nonpaying customers, I don't feel like that's it. Guys like that don't usually kill their clients or bury a ton of their targets in the same place. It allows for too much evidence to be easily found in one spot. But a serial killer? They get lost in the ritual, and they tend to operate in a more habitual way. I'll put some feelers out to our drug enforcement folks and get them to work that angle in case we're wrong, though. They'd have an ear to the ground that I don't."

*Smart.* Doing so would also allow someone else to follow that rabbit trail while they focused on the next lead.

They walked in a silence that was almost comfortable. That comfort was as disconcerting as the anxiety that had gnawed her since she pointed her SUV toward Virginia. *God, I want to live life like a normal person.*

She almost stopped walking. Since when did

she pray? Sure, she'd been raised in a Christian family and had attended a private Christian school. She'd grown up firm in her faith until God left her to fend for herself. There was no reason to appeal to Someone Who had no interest in protecting her.

Clenching her jaw, she surveyed the area and forced her brain to stop any thoughts of an ongoing conversation with the Man on a big throne upstairs.

She scanned the old Millionaires' Row, where the owners of the Pocahontas Coal Mine had once lived. Some of the houses were beautifully restored. Others had fallen into disrepair, the owners and tenants unable to keep up with the demands of maintaining a historic home. The town was a study in contrasts, of old and new, of past and present, of wealth and poverty.

They stopped in front of a house that rested somewhere between repair and disrepair. It was clear whoever lived there was working to restore the place to its former glory. It was also clear the work was moving slowly.

Noah raised a hand to knock on the door. "Let's hope someone's home." He knocked three times then stepped back beside her.

The floors creaked under heavy footsteps, and a man tugged the door open. Short and round, he appeared to be in his early sixties. His paint-stained T-shirt and worn work pants said he'd been busy at an interior restoration job. When he spotted Kelsie, he stared a little too long and his face showed a little too much interest.

Her stomach recoiled.

The man dragged his gaze from her as he wiped his hands on a rag and eyed Noah with suspicion. "Can I help you?"

The words were friendly. The tone was not.

Noah held up his credentials and identified himself, and the man straightened. Tough to tell if he was on guard or simply uneasy. After a couple of preliminary questions, Noah held up his phone. "Do you know this man?"

No flash of recognition appeared on the man's face. "No. Who is he?"

Glancing at the photo, Noah shoved the phone into his coat pocket. "He used your address on an employment application."

"Let me see it again." When Noah held up the phone, the man studied the photo then shook his head. "Look, I used to rent out rooms short-term, like people coming to ride the trails or get away from their lives. It's possible he was here then, but he doesn't ring no bells. If you give me his name, I can go take a look, maybe get back to you later." He backed away, his forehead creasing. "Should I be worried? He kill somebody?"

Noah shook his head as he pulled out a card and handed it over. "He's no danger to anyone. We're looking for some more information about him. If you find anything in your records, please email or call me."

When they were back on the sidewalk, Noah turned away from where they'd parked and started walking.

Kelsie hesitated before following. She really wanted to get out of town, not prolong their visit. "What are we doing?"

"I want to take a walk along the old road between these houses and the river and get a look at the back of the house, make sure we aren't missing anything."

It made sense, and she should have thought of it first. Was she off her game? She was good at what she did, one of the best investigators at Trinity. That was why Elliott had hired her.

Silently, they rounded the corner by the old stone church.

Kelsie shivered. "I know this is supposed to be beautiful, but it always kind of creeped me out." The dark stone structure sat on a small lawn. Gray skies above and the chill in the air made the place feel slightly sinister, even if it was a house of God.

Maybe that was the problem.

"I remember." Noah's voice was low as they turned onto the narrow road that had likely once been a drive for carriages or cars. "It always gave you the heebies."

Kelsie shoved her hands into her pockets. She didn't want to remember. She didn't want *him* to remember. And she certainly didn't want her heart to warm slightly at the fact he remembered.

Yet it did.

They neared the back of the house as another ATV engine revved nearby, headed for the trails.

"Snow's late this year, so the trails are more active." Noah slowed as he approached the house, eyeing the windows in the back. Nothing seemed out of place. It was just a nondescript older house that clearly needed work. He shrugged. "It's a bust. I don't see any—"

The ATV engine revved higher and roared closer.

Kelsie whirled toward the sound.

A four-wheeler, the driver dressed in thick pants and a heavy jacket, features hidden behind a full-face helmet with a dark visor, raced up the narrow street, aiming straight for Noah.

# SIX

"Noah!" Kelsie reflexively screamed his name.

He was already diving out of the way.

The ATV veered in Noah's direction and clipped his leg. He rolled toward the fence along the backyard of the house.

As it pulled out of the swerve, the ATV skidded and nearly lost control, slowing as the driver tried to regain traction.

Kelsie's throat nearly closed as Noah lay still against the fence. Was he okay? Had he—

"Kelsie, go!" Waving his hand, he suddenly pushed up to one knee.

Help Noah? Or chase the ATV on foot?

She was on the run before she could think it through, gaining on the four-wheeler as it spun tires in the wet grass along the side of the road. She reached out, her fingers brushing the metal on the rear of the vehicle before the tires caught traction, flinging mud and dead grass everywhere, and roared away. The vehicle skidded around the turn at the end of the street, the sound of its engine fading into the distance.

Spitting out grass and swiping mud from her face and coat, Kelsie fought the urge to stomp her foot like a two-year-old and to say words she still didn't allow herself to say, even if she wasn't on speaking terms with Jesus.

There was no way to catch the ATV and its driver. Heart racing, she jogged to Noah, who had pulled himself up to a seated position and was leaning on the fence.

The side of his black jacket was coated in mud. His dark jeans were smeared with dirt at the left hip. He was breathing heavily.

But he was alive.

Dropping beside him, Kelsie reached out to touch his shoulder but stopped with her hand hovering between them. "Are you hurt?"

"Not any worse than getting tackled in football." He rolled his head from one side to the other and lifted his shoulders before dropping them again. "I don't think anything's jacked up too bad, but it's going to bruise."

Was he telling her the truth, or was he in more pain than he was letting on? While the ATV hadn't slammed into him, the glancing blow had been enough to throw him to the ground.

A direct hit could have killed him.

How would she have handled that? She'd have

been feet away if he'd been seriously injured or worse.

*Twice.* Twice she'd been in a position to protect him. Twice she'd failed. Once her fear had slowed her reactions and prevented her from apprehending a possible killer. Now her best efforts hadn't been enough to stop the attack.

She rocked back on her heels and stared at him. She couldn't save him, and she'd been right beside him. *What if...*

What if he'd been with her that night and she'd still—

She wanted to press her palms to her ears and scream to keep back the whisper. *Beautiful ballerina.* It was still there. It was always there. And it was louder in this place than it had been since the first memory resurfaced through the fog.

She dug her fingers into her knees to still her shaking fingers. What if, in spite of Noah's love for her and his desire to protect her, he couldn't? What if—

"I said I'm fine. You can stop staring at me like you expect my brain to leak out of my eyeballs or something." Noah's grumble jerked her into the present.

She filled her lungs with damp, cold air and exhaled slowly, focusing on the pressure of her fingers digging into her knees. *Focus, Kelsie. Focus.*

There was no time to get lost in the past. That ATV could roar up for round two at any second, and they had nowhere to run if it did. They had to get out of here, back into her SUV and back to safety.

She couldn't fail Noah again.

She stood and reached out a hand to help him up.

Neither of them had worn gloves despite the cold, and his skin was warm against hers, the sensation achingly familiar. Their palms slid together in a way both safe and shocking. Kelsie tried to ignore it as she dug in her heels while Noah pulled himself to his feet.

When he was upright and steady, he didn't let go.

Neither did she.

His touch pulled her back to the night of their junior prom, when she'd been driving his truck to the school. He'd reached across the pickup's bench seat and inexplicably taken her hand for the first time ever. No words. No explanations. He'd just...held her hand.

It had been pure, perfect and thrilling. Warm and right and heart-racingly different.

She'd loved every second of the emotions she hadn't realized she'd been feeling until that moment. And then, because of some unspoken *thing* in the air between them, she'd pulled off at an overlook and looked over at him, their gazes locking. Noah had pressed the button to release her seat belt, pulled her across the bench seat to him and kissed her for the first time.

Everything had changed. The love building between them had settled into its rightful place, right there in his pickup truck with the sunset pouring golden approval over them.

Life had been bright and perfect. They'd lived in the warmth of that sunset for over a year...

Until her world went dark.

Kelsie jerked her hand from his and swiped it against her thigh, trying to wipe away his touch and the memories it contained.

Noah pretended not to notice, but the light that died in his eyes said he hadn't missed a thing.

Kelsie started walking. "We need to get out of here. Can you walk?"

"I'm fine." His voice was hard, and he set out at a brisk pace, passing her, not looking to the right or to the left. His hand hovered near his right hip, where she knew his sidearm was holstered, and he barely limped, though it was clear he was feeling at least a little pain.

She followed, scanning the street, the river and the houses. Bramwell was relatively quiet. Most ATVers had hit the trail earlier and would be back for lunch soon. There was little else to draw people during the cold of January after the Christmas house tours were over.

Was the sleepy town hiding something sinister? Were the other victims also from the area? Was a killer hunting along the trails?

And why was Noah in the crosshairs? That ATV driver hadn't been interested in her. Noah had been the target. Why would someone come after him?

*Unless...*

Unless someone had figured out who Noah Cross really was. Even she wasn't supposed to know his family's deepest secret. If someone else had found out, then—

"Say something." Noah strode on, the limp lessening as he loosened up.

She couldn't. Not here. Not now. Not out loud where anyone could hear. No, she had to shove this into her hip pocket until it was safe to speak.

What did he want her to say anyway? Did he want to hear her thoughts about the attacks? The way his touch had lit a fire in her heart that she couldn't seem to put out?

Her cheeks heated. No, they could never talk about that.

Things between them were too tight, too tense. No matter what the past looked like, no matter how conflicted she was about the present, they were working together, and there had to be some way to defuse the tension between them. She sniffed and went for the most innocuous comment she could find. "You never played football."

"What?" He stopped and turned to her, his face an odd blend of annoyance and confusion. "What are you talking about?"

Forcing a smile, she crowbarred a teasing note into her voice. "You said you felt like you got tackled in football. How would you know what that felt like? We didn't even have a football team. You get tackled on the bleachers at a basketball game or something?"

His cheeks puffed as he exhaled and turned away, muttering under his breath. He stopped at the sidewalk, looking up and down Main Street before he stepped off the curb to cross to her SUV. "You vex me, woman."

Kelsie kept a close eye on the street, her ears attuned to the sounds of approaching engines, though the only vehicles seemed to be moving on Bloch Road at the far end of Main Street. She waited until they were in her SUV with the doors shut before she looked at him. "I *vex* you? How old are you? Ninety?"

He sniffed and stared out the window as she pulled out of the gravel lot past the museum and out of town. They followed the river for a bit, and the silence grew heavier with each mile.

Either he was knee-deep in his feelings, or he was puzzling through the information they'd learned today. There was a lot, yet there was nothing. Thus far, there was little to jeopardize the verdict against Trenton Daniels, but they were on shaky ground when it came to reasonable doubt. At the very least, she couldn't give Elliott any answers until they knew times of death on the buried victims.

Kelsie had other questions as well. Who was coming after Noah and why? Two attempts on his life in less than twenty-four hours was more than a coincidence. The questions needed to be asked, although they'd broach a topic the two of them had discussed once and never again. "Noah?"

"What?" His voice was clipped.

She'd interrupted his thought process, but maybe it needed to be interrupted. "Do you feel secure talking openly with me right now? In this vehicle? Phones off?"

His head whipped toward her, his expression all sharp edges. Did he have an idea where she was going? Shutting off their phones was a risky move when someone was clearly coming after him, but it would only be for a moment, and she needed him to think about some things he might be avoiding.

Would he do it?

He swallowed so hard she could hear it, and he never looked away from her. She'd probably driven two miles before he pulled his phone from his pocket and shut it off. Reaching for hers in the bracket on her cupholder, he shut it down as well.

It was a dangerous move. They couldn't be reached. They would be incredibly difficult to track. But they also couldn't be overheard.

They were, for all intents and purposes, truly alone.

Whatever this conversation was, he wasn't sure he wanted to be involved.

On the flip side, she was showing him the kind

of trust she hadn't offered since she'd vanished. Did she realize she'd placed herself in a position where she couldn't call for help?

He wasn't sure whether to be honored or angry.

Either way, they needed to be quick. Having his cell phone off during an active investigation when Val might need to reach him was risky business. "What do you want to discuss?"

Kelsie tapped the steering wheel with her thumbs, seeming reluctant to speak. Finally, she reached a straight stretch of road and looked over at him. "You."

He pointed at his chest, eyebrow arched. All this time she'd been acting completely out of character and had left behind an SAT test's worth of questions, yet she wanted to talk about *him*?

"A possible serial killer is one thing, and we obviously need to dig deeper." Kelsie chewed her lower lip, a move he'd seen a thousand times when she was nervous about a performance or life in general.

She'd done it a lot in their last few days together, likely concerned about moving to New York. Or maybe she'd picked up on his reluctance to let her go, on his thoughts about going into law enforcement wherever she went.

Was *that* what she wanted to talk about?

"Noah, somebody is out to get you. It's clear you're a target, but we're not talking about it. Your house, now—"

"I've worked a lot of cases and made a lot of enemies. Even when I was on patrol, before I moved into investigations, I had a ton of people who might not want me to see another birthday. You know how it goes, I'm sure."

"I do." A shadow passed over her expression. "I put in some time in the army as a military police officer." Her voice was low.

*Wow.* He hadn't seen that coming. "The army? As an MP? What happened to ballet? What happened to make you—"

"That's not the point. The point is you. Noah, we both know people kill for a lot of reasons. Greed, anger..." She looked away from the road long enough to pin his gaze. "Revenge."

In a rush of terrified heat, he knew exactly where this discussion was headed. His whole life had been lived with one fear and one fear only. That fear had chased him and his family across the country, and it still wormed its way into his nightmares, even though over twenty years had passed. Even though Jack Rollins had died in prison four years earlier.

Though the threat was essentially over, it was still something that should never be discussed, not when Rollins had associates who were still out in the world. "We can't talk about this." He'd told her his story back when he was young and thought he knew better than the "grownups," against the primary rule of witness protection and against every promise he'd been forced to make to his parents and to the US Marshals. He'd sworn her to secrecy and to never speak of it again.

Now here she was, waltzing back into his life and speaking of it.

"But we need to. Noah, you have to ask yourself if it's possible someone has figured out who you are. And if that's the case..."

She didn't need to finish the sentence. *If that's the case*, then there was a lot more at stake than solving a crime.

His entire family could be in danger.

Kelsie was quiet, probably letting reality sink in. Even now, isolated in her car with their phones shut down, she was being careful not to say anything obvious, for which he was incredibly grateful. With witness protection, one could never be too careful. "Jack Rollins is dead. While there's a remote chance one of his—"

"Even a remote chance is a chance."

That was the last thing he wanted to admit. He'd grown used to feeling a sense of freedom. Had it all been false? "If you're right, that would require me to make some phone calls that would upend some lives."

"So we need to be certain before we pull any triggers."

*Deadly* certain. One phone call to the US Marshals would have his parents whisked away from their comfortable life in Shiloh Peak, where they ran a store that sold rafting, camping and climbing gear. One phone call would pull his brother and brand-new wife out of his graduate program at UVA. One phone call would take Noah off this case, out of this state, and out of law enforcement forever.

He'd assumed the threat had died with Jack Rollins, but what if it hadn't?

This time, *Kelsie* was going to have to pull off to the side of the road because *he* was going to be sick.

Noah pulled in measured deep breaths, trying to keep himself focused on the now, because the past was about to steamroll him into the ground.

It would be his sixth-grade year all over again, when he'd been forced to leave everything he knew in Seattle, including his name, to move to what he'd derisively referred to as "the backwoods of Virginia." He'd been arrogant and angry, rebellious to the core. At a time when his family was dealing with stress and trauma in the wake of his father testifying against his boss, Noah had piled on the pain.

By eighth grade, he'd been on the train to yet another expulsion or worse. But then he'd been paired with the goody-two-shoes ballet kid on a history project. A very long day trip to Jamestown with her parents had ended when they pulled into his parents' driveway around midnight, and he got out of the car with a brand-new best friend. In tenth grade, on a hike in the middle of nowhere, he'd sworn her to secrecy and told her the truth about who he was and where he'd come from, making her promise never to discuss it again.

She'd been an even better friend after that. And she'd held to the promise until now, when she came close to speaking his worst fears aloud.

Noah exhaled, begging God to settle his insides so he could think like a reasonable adult in law enforcement and not a terrified middle schooler in chaos. "For now, we don't jump to conclusions. Nobody else I know has been targeted, and that would be odd." Did she hear what he was saying? If someone had found him and figured out he was his father's son, then the short leap to his father would be easy to make. If someone in Jack Rollins's circle was harboring anger decades later, they'd go after Noah's father, or they'd go after the easier target in Noah's brother. Taking aim at the veteran law enforcement officer first would be a risky move.

Besides, his attacker at the house had been wearing the same coveralls as the person who'd been burying Jaxon Collins in Burke's Garden. Unless they were randomly dealing with a hired gun who'd happened to recognize him, that puzzle piece didn't fit with the Rollins crew and revenge.

That truth settled into Noah's chest and brought vague relief. While someone was out to get him, it likely wasn't because of his family.

He prayed it wasn't because of his family.

The slim possibility that the past might be stalking them still demanded he take action, just in case. He reached for his phone but didn't turn it on as he processed what should come next. "I think the safe bet is for someone to take a short vacation without planning a big extended trip yet." His parents could close the store for a week or so and go out of town. His brother's semester hadn't started yet. A second honeymoon might be in order.

There had been a couple of spontaneous vacations when he was younger that he'd later learned had been planned out of an abundance of caution when someone suspicious rolled into town. It wouldn't be unusual for his family to take a breather until they knew whether they needed to pull up stakes on a move that would irrevocably change all of their lives. "I'll reach out when I feel like it's safe, and we'll handle it." They had a way of communicating that would let him speak freely without risking someone having access to his cell phone. Even with it off, they were still talking in riddles.

Kelsie nodded, clearly relieved to have the conversation behind them.

She looked softer somehow, as though concern for him and his family had melted some of the sharp edges she'd been cutting him with. If that was the case, maybe he could ask his own burning question while they were riding along in a communications blackout.

Did he dare? It was a small thing, something that shouldn't bother him, but it gnawed at his gut. "So why didn't you let me bring you dinner last night?" There it was. No preamble. No chance for her to plan and evade. He eyed her closely as he waited for an answer.

Her face visibly paled. Some of those edges sharpened her features again, as though she was building up a defense against something only she could see. Her chin tilted up, and she seemed to wrestle with how to breathe. It took her a few seconds to respond. "A few months ago, a friend of mine had her life threatened, and it turned out to be someone she trusted, someone close to her. She's deathly allergic to peanuts, and they managed to slip enough into her food to take her out." Her voice shook slightly. "I guess it taught me you can't be too careful. Not even with the people you trust." The last words came out as thin as a razor's edge.

He didn't buy her story. While he didn't think she was lying, there was more to this than she was saying. He hadn't gotten this far in his career without trusting his instincts and his five senses, without a brain that thought through clues with methodical order. What she was saying might be true, but it didn't explain her behavior.

No. Whatever trust issues she had, they ran

deeper than something happening *to a friend.* They were personal.

And they somehow involved him.

Without taking her eyes from the road, she pulled her phone from the cradle and passed it to him. "Turn that on, please."

In other words, like a line he'd once seen on an old sitcom, *I'm done talking to you now.*

Pushing her would only cause her to retreat, so he fired up her phone then settled it back into place. Feeling oddly defeated, he powered his up as well.

A missed call and a voicemail immediately popped onto the screen.

*Val.*

She never called to chat. She'd only be reaching out if there was news on the case.

Call me as soon as you're in range. We caught a break.

# SEVEN

How long before they were off this winding two-lane road? She needed a straight stretch of highway where she could floor it until they reached a place where she could get out of this SUV and away from Noah.

When things had felt like they might be slightly comfortable, he'd had to go and ask a question she couldn't answer. At least, she couldn't answer without telling the truth.

It wasn't that she'd lied. Seeing her teammate Rebecca stricken by a hidden poison had unnerved her. The repeated attacks on one of the few people Kelsie called *friend* had unlocked the doors and allowed all of her fears to rush forward. She'd had to drill down to the most hardened parts of herself in order to get through that time, and she'd only managed to do it by focusing solely on Rebecca's safety, shoving aside any fears for herself or dark memories from her past.

Rebecca's case had hit too close to home. It had sent Kelsie running on a two-week sabbatical to the coast, claiming she needed a vacation. The alone time on tiny Ocracoke Island had helped to quiet her mind and emotions, but it clearly hadn't been enough to heal her.

Coming home had been plain foolish. She'd thought she could face the past head-on and defeat it with sheer strength and willpower. It was what she'd trained to do.

Well, she'd been wrong. The past was blowing holes in her defenses, and it threatened to cripple her.

Now Noah was skirting the barbed-wire fence and creeping uncomfortably close to the truth, asking questions she never wanted to answer. So yes, while Rebecca's case had thrown her for a loop, Noah could not have any idea what the real issue was.

The core of her heart still blamed him for not being there to stop the evil she'd been helpless to stop on her own.

Powerless. Shamed. Shattered.

It took all of her willpower not to yank the wheel, screech the car to a halt on the side of the road in a hail of gravel and run screaming into the woods.

She couldn't do that. She was Kelsie McIlheney. Former soldier. Muay Thai practitioner. Accomplished investigator.

Nothing could defeat her.

Nothing.

Maybe if she kept repeating it, she'd believe it. That had worked in the past, but the past had never been so close.

Noah had gone back to his phone and didn't seem to notice she was wrestling for her very life. The passenger seat was quiet.

Too quiet.

When she glanced over, he was tapping his screen, his face drawn in deep concentration.

She had to break the brittle silence. "Is everything okay?"

He barely spared her a look. "Not sure. Val says we might have a break but, of course, we're in a dead zone. I can't get a call out. I had signal long enough to get her text and voicemail."

Ironic, given they'd shut their phones off in an extremely cautious effort to make sure no one could tap into their conversation. Of course, the important info had come in during the two minutes they'd been out of reach.

But a break in the case? Discovering who was trying to bury Jaxon Collins and who had buried the other remains might allow her to resume her look into the case against Trenton Daniels. It might get her out of the mountains faster.

She willed his phone to find a tower. Maybe even dared to pray a little. It seemed home turf was drawing out old habits.

But was prayer an *old habit*? Or was it something more? Maybe—

"Val. What have you got?" Noah had put the phone to his ear and was firing out terse *yes* and *no* responses, leaving no clue to what was happening on the other side of the conversation. "Send me what you have. We'll meet you there. You take lead." He lowered the phone but continued to stare at the screen.

Kelsie was dying to ask what he'd learned, but it wasn't her place. While the state was allowing her to tag along because of the close proximity to the Trenton Daniels case, they were under no obligation to pass along new information. She kept her mouth shut and tried to prevent her bubbling questions from bursting forth.

Noah never looked up from his phone. "There's an old coal preparation plant over the border in Virginia, not far from here. It's been abandoned for decades, condemned. State keeps trying to auction it off, but the buyer would have to drop a small fortune in order to clean up the site, so it's sitting there. Val says the lab found residue on some of the remains from Burke's Garden that is consistent with what would be found in a coal preparation plant."

"I remember the place." While she'd been a fairly quiet kid, focused on school and on her mother's dream of having her dance with the American Ballet Theater, she hadn't been ignorant. She'd not been the partying type, but some of the other kids from surrounding high schools had regularly thrown ragers at the old coal prep plant.

Some of the kids had sought fun and found trouble.

Kelsie had largely stayed away from those parties, yet trouble had still found her.

She gripped the steering wheel. She hadn't thought so much about the past in years. Coming back had been the worst decision of her life.

Well, the second worst.

"Val's going to meet us there to take a look, see about bringing in techs. It might be nothing, because we're working on what amounts to the law of averages here."

It made sense though. "Lab finds traces consistent with coal prep, but you eliminate all active sites and go for the closest inactive one to the burial site?" If a serial killer was holding his victims before murdering them or was looking for a place to hide, he wouldn't operate in an area frequented by others. An abandoned plant in the middle of nowhere would offer a perfect place to kill.

It was doubtful they'd find their bad guy onsite. The killer knew he'd been spotted and they were on the hunt, so he'd likely gone underground, at least for the moment. Still, if he was operating out of the plant, the scene might yield a wealth of clues that could identify the perpetrator or more of his victims.

It might also yield a clue as to who was targeting Noah and why. She sincerely hoped it had nothing to do with his parents.

They hit a drive-through and ate on the road. Kelsie wasn't hungry, and her stomach was definitely threatening a full-on rebellion, but she couldn't let herself drop as low as she had yesterday, not if she wanted to keep her faculties at full strength. A burger crammed in on the run and chased by a Coke would have to do.

When they rolled up to the site, an unmarked SUV and a pickup truck bearing the logo of a local security company sat in the small overgrown parking lot. The asphalt was cracked by weeds that had taken over and obliterated the parking spaces. A fence ran along the edge of the lot and around the land on which the plant sat. Barbed wire coiled along the tops of the chain-link barrier. Offices and outbuildings stood near the parking lot on the other side of the fence, windows busted and doors hanging off their hinges.

Beyond the fences, huge coal chutes were strung several stories in the air between prep buildings and over storage areas where the ground was still dark with coal dust. An abandoned train engine sat on railroad tracks that had once ferried countless carloads of coal. Broken railroad tracks ran along the side of the site, overgrown and disjointed from lack of use. A small creek bubbled at the bottom of a ravine beyond the tracks, the edges icing over in the January cold.

Clouds hung low and heavy. The property was dreary, dark and depressing. Even the air felt stale and abandoned.

It was midafternoon, and the plant was a giant creepfest. After dark, this place was probably terrifying, something straight out of a horror movie.

For the killer's victims, it may have been the living embodiment of a horror movie, the place where they'd breathed their last terrified breaths. Had they been tortured slowly? Killed quickly? The medical examiner had yet to offer a cause of death for any of the victims, so the details were left to nightmares.

Kelsie shuddered as she shut the door of her SUV and drew her windbreaker tighter around her. Should she carry her gun? She was confident in her skills in a fight, but she wasn't fond of going up against a serial killer without something to protect herself from surprises.

Then again, Noah had his. Val had hers. The security guard likely had one as well. They might not be too thrilled about her adding another firearm to the mix.

Against her better judgment, she'd refrain.

Val joined them and looked at Kelsie as though she was unsure about her presence, then offered a wry smile. "You two look like you've been slogging through a swamp."

Kelsie winced. She'd forgotten about the mud

the ATV had splashed on her and the grass stains from Noah's roadside dive.

"Long story." Noah brushed off the comment. "What's going on here?"

"We haven't seen any movement. From here, it doesn't appear anyone is on the property or in the surrounding area, so hopefully we aren't looking at a confrontation." Val glanced at her phone as though she was reading notes, then pocketed the device. "Since this is basically based on an educated guess, we may be walking into a whole bunch of nothing."

"There are a few abandoned prep plants within a hundred square miles of us, but this one being close to the burial ground makes it our best start." Noah eyed the scene as though he was creating a map in his head. "Maybe to keep it from being a complete bust, we can take some shaky cell phone video and start our own urban explorer social media page."

"Funny you should say that." Val pulled her phone out again, typed on the screen and held it up for them to see a streaming video of the site. "The techs found a few amateur videos where people have been inside the buildings. The newest one is from a couple of years ago. There didn't seem to be much going on, but we'll go in and see for ourselves."

Kelsie said nothing, just followed as they approached the security guard who stood near a locked gate. This was a quiet operation, not the kind of geared-up move-out there would have been if they'd suspected a murderer was present.

Still, her heart pounded with anticipation of what might be inside the tall rusting metal buildings or what might lurk in the abandoned office and storage units.

Val was right. This location could be nothing... or it could be everything.

Their footsteps crunched on the gravel parking lot. A guard from the private company that secured the property unlocked the gate. He offered a nod as they entered. Val had secured permission from the property owner for them to investigate, so they were good to go.

Noah's heart beat with the anticipation of discovery...or confrontation. This could all be over in a minute, or they could be no closer to the end than they had been when they started.

Val stopped in front of the guard. "I know we spoke a few minutes ago, but can you tell Special Agent Cross what you told me?"

The man pulled his cap down tighter on his head. "Sure, but I'm afraid I'm not much help. The only people I've had to deal with are younger kids looking to throw a kegger or guys with cell phones looking to boost their hits online. Off the top of my head, I can't remember seeing any of their faces here more than once. And honestly, it's been quiet out here for a few years, ever since a kid broke his leg and they tightened up the perimeter."

Noah remembered the news story about the injured kid. A college frat had decided to throw a party and one of the guys had fallen off the old train engine. It was surprising an injury hadn't happened sooner. The place had been a party spot when Noah and Kelsie were in high school, though they'd never visited. Time and weather had degraded the buildings until it was clear they were a danger. "Do you share patrol of this site with anyone?" Noah wanted to speak to each person who had been here, see if anyone had noticed anything unusual.

"Just me. When traffic slowed down, we scaled back patrols. The owner cut way back on patrols and only has us drive by sporadically. For a while, we relied on cameras, but we took them down when we strengthened the fence a few years back. Owners didn't want to spend the money on monitoring cameras or on our hourly rate, I guess."

Cameras would have helped a great deal, and removing them probably wasn't smart. Fences were deterrents, but they didn't stop the determined.

This guy knew it, too. He offered a sheepish shrug. He was a worker, not the owner of the site or the company. He did as he was told.

Val stopped near the first building, a small shed

that had probably once been a security office or a welcome center. "Mr. Deekins and I will take the office buildings." Val pointed to the tall towers in the center of the property. "You guys want to start with the nearest one? We'll move on to the far one when we're done with the outbuildings."

"Works for me." Noah took a set of keys Deekins held out to him, then headed for the nearest tower with Kelsie keeping pace beside him.

This was not how he would have run things if he was in charge of the scene. He'd have never allowed Kelsie to be on point with him.

Kelsie existed in some weird limbo area where her organization had been hired by the state to look into a crime that dovetailed with this investigation, but she wasn't officially law enforcement. He could technically ask her to stay behind, and maybe he should.

Everything in him wanted to send her back to her vehicle to wait with the doors locked. That was the safest place on the property. Even after sixteen years, the instinct to protect her was alive and kicking. She had always been internally strong, able to handle the pressure her parents and her dance instructors placed on her and to do so with a smile. The physical strength she'd built as a dancer had made her appear long and graceful and almost wispy, leading to the illusion of fragile beauty. She was anything but fragile, yet he'd felt protective of her. Maybe that's what love did. Maybe it drove you to shield your loved one from harm.

So why was he driven to protect her now? He no longer loved her, no matter what his heart's memories tried to say. Besides, she was physically stronger than ever, as was evidenced by the way she'd handled herself the day before. She still moved like a dancer, but raw steel infused her very being. There was a tension coiled inside her that was ready to spring. Kelsie was trained to fight, and she was probably lethal even without a gun strapped at her hip.

*Hmm.* Maybe he wanted her at his side after all.

He forced himself to focus as they reached the first structure. It towered over them, a hulking blue metal monster that waited to devour all who dared to approach. They circled the perimeter then entered through a door hanging open on rusty hinges.

The interior was vast and largely empty. It smelled of old damp coal, the sulfuric fumes almost more than he could handle. Saying little, they shone their flashlights around the space, the beams glancing off cobwebs and highlighting animal droppings. Nothing seemed to be disturbed.

Kelsie headed for the door first. "This place is a heap. We're more likely to run into a raccoon or a nest of black widows than a killer." She reached the murky daylight several feet ahead of him.

Noah almost smiled. Ah, yes. Kelsie hated spiders as much as he hated mice.

*Wait.* His smile flipped. This place was probably crawling with rodents. And not just mice. There were probably rats.

*That* wasn't the image he needed in his head. He stopped himself from scanning the ground for traces of "rodents of unusual size" and focused on looking for footprints, fibers or anything else that might indicate someone had been here recently.

They rounded the corner to the base of the grated metal stairs that clung to the side of the building and went all the way to the top.

They were in better shape than he'd expected. Although a few of the steps were broken at a corner weld, the majority seemed to be holding on.

"I'll go first." He'd have to step gingerly to make sure one didn't buckle under his weight, but if the metal could hold him, it could certainly hold Kelsie.

Slowly, they picked their way up, one step at a time. As the leader, he kept his eyes on the stairs while Kelsie watched the area around the facility. The few glances he took at their surroundings convinced him these stairs would be a great place to enjoy the view, to sit and pray, or to simply be quiet when a case hit too close to his heart.

Kind of like this one.

Kelsie had raised questions about the safety of his family, but he couldn't make that theory hold water. Whoever had attacked him at his house had worn the same coveralls as the person burying Jaxon Collins's remains. If this was about his father's testimony, then why would their suspect be killing other people instead of coming after his family?

No, this was about something else, something they had yet to uncover.

And he had other things to worry about. While someone was taking potshots at his life, Kelsie was tightening her grip on his heart. What would happen if they stopped this methodical climb up these stairs, sat together and spoke honestly about the past sixteen years? About the night when everything inexplicably changed?

"Noah?" Her voice came from a couple feet behind and below him.

Was she reading his thoughts? Did she want to talk?

He had to clear his throat to answer. "Yeah?" What if she did? What if now was the time—

"Don't look until you can make it appear casual, but I think I see movement off to the left, about a hundred yards up the mountain in a group of trees clumped together. It's tough to tell with the clouds muting the shadows and the breeze moving the branches."

His pulse picked up. Was the killer watching? Were they closer to answers than they'd anticipated? The murderer could be nearby, waiting to see if they located his hideaway.

Noah's breaths quickened, and it wasn't from the multistory climb. If the suspect truly wanted to take one of them out, it would only take one well-placed shot to kill—

"I could be wrong." Kelsie's voice was low, although the distance to the site she'd mentioned would have made eavesdropping impossible even if she'd shouted. "I'm not seeing anything now. Maybe I'm paranoid." The last words came out with a discouragement he hadn't thought her capable of. He'd seen her angry, even sad, but never defeated.

It was disconcerting and a little scary for reasons he didn't want to consider.

After what felt like an endless climb, they reached the top of the stairs. A grated landing offered access to a large metal door.

He definitely wasn't looking down. The ground was too far away. Next to mice, heights were his least favorite thing.

Noah inspected the lock on the door, then tried to appear nonchalant as he turned to speak to Kelsie, who had stepped up beside him. His gaze swept past her to the hill beyond, locating the stand of trees she'd mentioned. The trunks grew close together and created deep shadows, the perfect place for someone to pull surveillance or to set up a sniper's nest.

Nothing seemed to be amiss, at least not at first glance. "I'm not seeing anything, but give me a second."

When she nodded, his attention drifted to her. She was watching him, waiting to see if he saw something out of place.

Their eyes locked. It was the first time he'd looked at her this closely, close enough to see the flecks of darker blue in her eyes. Close enough to remember every single time he'd ever stared into her eyes before.

Right before he'd kissed her. Or right before she'd kissed him.

The last time he'd been this close to her, they'd definitely shared a kiss, the kind that left his brain scrambled and his heart certain she was the only woman he could ever lo—

*Dude.* What was wrong with him? He jerked his chin to break the connection. The motion ripped his gaze from hers and doused the heat that blasted past his heart. There was a probable serial killer on the loose, and he was a target. Getting lost in Kelsie's eyes was the absolute last thing he should be doing.

For about ten million reasons.

He ignored the zing under his skin and reached for the keys he'd pocketed when Deekins had handed them over. This door was padlocked. Based on the intel Val had sent and that he'd reviewed while they were driving to the site, there weren't many places to hide at the plant, but—

"Stop. Look up. Above the door." Kelsie's voice was low but urgent.

Noah froze with his fingers gripping the keys in his pocket then tipped his head back.

Above the door frame, a mounting bracket had been bolted to the wall. Unlike the surrounding metal, which had aged from years of exposure to the elements, the bracket was relatively clean. Given the marks in the rust and dirt around it, it had been touched recently. "Camera mount?"

"Possibly." Kelsie was being very quiet. The few words she spoke were efficient and quick. Likely, she was focused on looking for clues.

As he should be.

Because if there had been a camera mounted here recently, they might have found their suspect's killing ground.

# EIGHT

Everything about this place gave her the creeps, but fearful anticipation hadn't shivered down Kelsie's spine until she'd spotted that bracket. It clearly hadn't been exposed to the weather for very long.

A new bracket meant a camera had been here recently, and a camera meant—

"Well, this is definitely not something the security company installed." Noah pulled his phone from his pocket and snapped a photo then texted something, probably to Val. Then he pocketed the device again. "Deekins said they'd removed all the cameras. I saw the framework for some on the outbuildings. They held the big, clunky professional surveillance cameras. This one is smaller, like for one of those webcams people put around their houses." He smirked. "Probably something I should do."

*Definitely* something he should do. One assault at his house was enough. Cameras might have given him warning and could have provided answers they needed to put an end to this.

Cameras might have saved her at one time, too, or at least given her answers to who—

She shuddered, then set a neutral expression onto her face when Noah offered her a pair of latex gloves he'd pulled from his pocket. She was careful not to touch his fingers. That look, that *moment*, that had passed between them had torn a few more bricks out of the wall around her heart.

As she tugged the gloves on, she forced her focus to the mounting bracket. "Those require internet to transmit. If our bad guy was relying on them, then he had to have some method of getting a signal."

Noah pulled the keys from his pocket and eyed the padlock. "They could have set up a satellite system. They're fairly simple to set up. We'll take a look at the companies that service the area, see if we get a hit on anyone using one out here."

*Smart.* It might take time to cut through the red tape and get the records though. Providers could be notoriously protective of their data. Trinity could help. Elliott had a way of dealing with red tape, and she didn't ask questions.

Noah crouched by the door, flipping through the keys on the ring. He stopped and looked up at her. "Guess what."

"No key matches that padlock?" Her heart thumped harder. If someone had changed the lock, it was further evidence they were in the right place.

She could pick the lock, but she wasn't sure she wanted to let Noah know she had that particular set of skills. It seemed a little on the nose for a PI.

But Noah never stopped moving. He tugged at his gloves, inspected the lock, then reached into his interior jacket pocket and pulled out a small case.

As it turned out, Noah Cross had his own particular set of skills. It only took a minute for him to pop the lock and pocket his gear. "Bingo." He stood, opened the door and, after a quick glance at her, stepped across the threshold into the darkness.

Kelsie followed, pausing to hook the door to an anchor on the railing to hold it open. There was no way she was getting trapped in the dark.

The small anteroom held the air of a closed crypt. There were no windows. The walls were the same metal as the exterior of the building. If the door had been closed, the room would have been unbearably dark, enclosed and still. Only the fresh air and murky light that poured through the open doorway diluted the heavy, musty dampness.

They clicked on their flashlights and swept the space.

Noah inhaled deeply. "This is definitely different than the rest of the building."

The air was disturbed, as though someone had

been here recently, although Kelsie couldn't explain the source of the sensation. Unlike the downstairs, the space was free of cobwebs and dust, as though it had been recently swept.

Someone was trying to cover their tracks, to clean up evidence.

Noah aimed his light at a door a few feet away, his footfalls echoing on the metal as he stepped closer.

Caution signs were affixed to the metal door. *High Voltage. Authorized Personnel Only.* They were worn and had been there for a while. Their presence should be enough to cause even the bravest "urban explorer" to pause.

They virtually ensured the door would remain untouched, offering the perfect place to hide...or to hide someone.

Noah motioned for her to stand to the side as he reached for the doorknob. It was the only door they'd encountered that wasn't padlocked. It had a handle and what appeared to be a dead bolt that was not original to the door.

*Interesting.*

"Bet you don't have a key for that either." But she did. Kelsie tilted her head from side to side. Anxiety was building. The dark, the thought of being imprisoned...it was starting to play with her head. She needed to do something, take some action. "It's my turn to show off."

Noah stepped aside and motioned her forward.

Reaching into her pocket, she pulled out her own small case and removed a bump key. It made shorter work than picking, but only on certain types of locks. Inserting the key into the lock, she gave it a couple of taps and...

"Bingo." She pocketed the key and arched an eyebrow at Noah.

It looked like he might speak, but then his expression shifted and he rested his hand on his sidearm.

He was right. This wasn't the time to be flippant. Kelsie stepped back and gave him room to work.

Noah drew his weapon and held it low. "State police!" He pulled the door open and stepped inside.

Kelsie's heart hammered, waiting for the shout, the shot, the scuffle...

There was only silence.

She shifted sideways slowly, wishing she'd brought her gun after all. *One heartbeat. Two. Three.*

Noah appeared in the doorway, holstering his pistol. "No one's here, but..." His expression was grim. He pulled out his phone, fired off a text, then motioned toward the door. "You can look, but don't go inside. We're going to turn this over to the crime scene techs. I promise you... None of this looks like anything related to Trenton Daniels. This is something different, and it's a whole lot worse."

Swallowing hard, Kelsie moved to the door. Noah held his flashlight over her shoulder, illuminating the small room.

The space was maybe six feet square. Old electrical panels dominated the walls, and bright warning stickers seemed to glow in every direction.

But electricity wasn't the most dangerous thing.

Her stomach tried to escape through her throat.

In the center of the room, an old metal chair sat, heavy and solid. Someone had bolted it to the floor with heavy L brackets, sixteen in total, four on each leg. It wasn't going anywhere. The floor around the chair had been scrubbed recently and was devoid of the dust and dirt that layered the rest of the room.

Handcuffs dangled from the arms of the chair, which bore dings and dents that indicated someone had struggled against their restraints.

Noah swept the light around the room. "Somebody tried to clean up, probably took out a bunch of what could be used as evidence after we spotted them in Burke's Garden. They had to know we'd eventually find the place." He aimed his light toward a corner. "There was a camera mounted here, too. They were watching."

Her heart pounded. Her breaths came in stutters. Someone had been held prisoner here. Had been watched here. Had—

The light sparked on something in the corner farthest from the door.

"What was that?" Reaching over her shoulder, she grabbed Noah's wrist and directed it back toward the spot that had caught her attention. She leaned forward but didn't cross the threshold into the room.

The object was glass and cylindrical.

A syringe.

"They drugged their captives to keep them quiet and complacent." Noah muttered words that dripped with disgust.

*Drugged. Quiet. Complacent.*

The words pounded her skull.

Whoever had been held here had likely awakened in the deepest darkness with no frame of reference for time and space. They'd have been groggy and sick, unsure of what had happened, terrified out of their minds...

She knew the feeling.

She was going to be sick.

Whirling, Kelsie shoved Noah aside and headed for the exterior door. Though it was only feet away, it felt like miles. She burst into the cloud-dampened light and stopped her forward momentum by grabbing onto the rail.

*Be strong, Kelsie. Be strong. You were raised better. You were raised stronger.* Her mother's voice berated her across time.

Her entire body pulsed with every heartbeat. Darkness. Confusion. Silence.

A presence she couldn't see. A voice she could still hear.

*Beautiful ballerina.*

Noah's heart hit his throat as Kelsie burst out the door. She was moving so fast, she might flip over the fragile railing and hurtle to her death.

He dashed out to find her leaning over the side and pulling in air as though she'd survived a near-drowning.

What was going on?

The scene inside that room was horrifying, no doubt. It twisted his stomach to think what might have happened in that dark, claustrophobic space, what sorts of tortures might have been scrubbed from the floor beneath that chair. It took sheer willpower to stay in his analytical mind and out of his natural human emotions.

Had Kelsie jumped off the mental springboard into her emotions? Had something inside that room triggered the fear that seemed to pulse around her?

Noah closed the door and stood near her, giving her space to center herself but remaining close if she needed help.

Kelsie had always had a vivid imagination. Had it raced headlong into scenes of the horror movie that had happened inside those four walls?

He shook his head to stop his own mind from going to dark places and allowed his eyes to adjust to daylight. His hand reached out to touch Kelsie's back, but he let it hover. Would touching her spook her worse? Or would it ground her in reality?

He rested his hand lightly between her shoulder blades.

She flinched and stiffened. For a second, it seemed as though she'd move away, but then she leaned slightly into his touch, staring at the mountain on the far side of the plant.

Even through her coat, he could feel the sharpness of her breathing, as though she couldn't quite get her lungs to move air in and out efficiently.

Something was tormenting her, but he had no idea what it could be. There was so much he could say, but what words did she need to hear? What had caused the strongest person he knew to panic?

He'd spent a few moments this morning looking into Trinity Investigations, and it was clear they had handled some pretty serious cases, giving a second look into often heinous crimes. There were hints they were involved in an investigation into the tragic murder of a young father in coastal North Carolina. That particular case had stood out to him because, unlike most of Trinity's investigations, it was still open.

Clearly, Kelsie was no stranger to gory evidence and gruesome crime scenes, so what had triggered her now?

If only he knew how to comfort her. Slowly, Noah moved his hand back and forth between her shoulder blades, silently praying for her to find the peace she needed. Years ago, when he'd been lost and scared and angry, it had been Kelsie who had introduced him to Jesus, who'd taught him to pray. They'd even prayed together at times.

Funny, but her normally open faith seemed to be shuttered right now. Something had definitely changed her. Was it war? Was it her job?

Was there something about Virginia that had set her off? Was there a traumatic reason behind her flight from home sixteen years ago, her drastic life changes and the fear that seemed to surround her like a fog?

The landing shook with a gentle rhythm that indicated someone was climbing the stairs. Reluctantly, he pulled his hand from Kelsie's back and walked over to look down, although the height made his stomach swim.

Deekins had walked up to the first landing and was standing guard. Val must have sent him to help secure the scene.

Was that wise? The person who had imprisoned their victims in that small room had open access to the property. That alone could be enough to move Deekins into suspect territory.

"I'm going back down." Kelsie must have felt the movement as well, because she eased to his side, her posture straight and her expression tight.

"I'll wait in my car. You don't need me up here getting in the way."

"Actually..." His words caused her to stop two steps below him. As much as she was hurting, he needed her help. When she didn't turn to face him, he kept talking. "Do you mind keeping close to the gate, helping guard the scene?"

She looked down, saw Deekins, then nodded. "I hear you. I'll meet him there."

Her words were robotic and forced. She made her way down the stairs as though she carried a burden no one but her could see.

Something in Noah's heart crumbled. What had happened to Kelsie McIlheney? For years, he'd assumed she'd abandoned him in a search for bigger and better things.

But what if it was something more? What if she'd been running from things he couldn't begin to fathom?

The only trauma he could trace was the way her mother had demanded perfection and excellence, had driven Kelsie to practice until she collapsed, to perform until she dropped, to keep up her grades until she passed out in exhaustion.

Had she reached a breaking point and fled?

He trailed her down the stairs, watching as she paused to speak to Deekins then made her way to the bottom.

She'd always run to Noah, had always confided

in him. What had caused her to suddenly leave him behind?

"Special Agent Cross." Deekins addressed him when they met on the lowest landing. "Special Agent Yewell sent me to guard the scene. She's called the techs and is waiting for them in the parking lot. She'll meet you there."

"Sounds good, but I'm going to have you wait by the gate with Ms. McIlheney." That would keep him at a distance from the actual crime scene and would keep him in sight from the parking lot. Noah suddenly didn't want to leave Kelsie alone with this man, although Deekins didn't seem to be the sort to harm her.

Still, one could never tell.

As he followed Deekins down the last flight of stairs, he looked over the room again in his mind's eye. Inside that room, despite someone's best efforts to strip it of evidence, there had to be something to lead them to the perpetrator. DNA on the chair, on the syringe, or—

His feet refused to take another step.

*The syringe.* It was, from a distance, exactly like the one in his hallway.

His stomach looped over itself, sending a wave of vertigo through him.

How close had he come to being the next inmate in that sick prison cell? To being locked away in there even at this moment?

He looked up at the heavy clouds and inhaled

air so cold it stung his throat. The fresh air was a stark contrast to what had likely become a tomb for at least one of the killer's victims.

What had they endured, breathing the stale air in the complete darkness of a metal room with no ventilation, no light? How many times had they been drugged into lethargy and silence? How helpless and terrified had they felt as their consciousness faded and their reality distorted?

The sickness that had soured his gut for too many hours spiked. The disorientation, the fear, the scent of death lingering so close... All of it had to have been more than any human being could handle.

And it could have been him.

This was straight out of a nightmare, a horror movie...or so much worse. He'd investigated horrible bloody murder scenes. He'd analyzed the aftermath of death in dozens of gruesome images.

But he'd never been so close to being the victim. He'd never had to place himself in the chair, with the restraints digging into his skin and his mind completely scrambled by Rohypnol and darkness.

He needed to get himself together.

With a shuddering breath, he walked around the corner of the building, away from curious eyes that might be watching from the parking lot.

No wonder Kelsie had freaked out. He was doing the exact same thing.

He leaned against the cold metal and took deep

breaths until he felt his mind settle enough to pray. He stared across the weed-strewn ground toward the mountain beyond. *Lord, I'm not sure what's happening, but I need you. Pretty sure Kelsie does, too. Make this make sense. Make—*

Movement to his left, toward the fence surrounding the property, cut the prayer short.

He whipped toward the motion, scanning the chain-link fence topped with barbed wire about ten yards away. He eyed the slumbering trees, the dead leaves and the undergrowth. Maybe it had been the breeze?

But no. While the wind had been moving pretty good up on the stairs, the terrain at ground level sheltered the area where he'd seen motion. Nothing stirred there.

Maybe it was his imagination. He was emotionally amped, short on sleep, high on adrenaline, and—

A shadow shifted from one clump of underbrush to the next. It was a person, crouched low, moving quickly.

He reached for his weapon and started sprinting. "I've got a runner!"

The figure gave up any pretense of hiding. They popped out of the underbrush and bolted east, a camouflage hunting jacket and pants making it tough to track them in the leaves.

How was he supposed to get past the fence and into the woods?

From the parking lot, shouts rose.

Noah stopped at the fence and waved toward Deekins as Val joined the guard. "Find a way past the fence! They're headed toward you!"

The pair ran toward the parking lot, where the fence came to an end and they could round it.

Where was Kelsie? Had she gone back to her vehicle?

There wasn't time to worry about that now. He had to focus.

It could be a spooked hunter or a curious teenager, but it could also be a killer who'd been surprised cleaning out his lair when they rolled up.

Noah sprinted down the fence line, trying to keep the shadow in sight, but he lost contact when the person took a hard right and dashed up the hill, disappearing into the trees.

Noah stopped to look for an indication of where the person had gone.

There was nothing.

He huffed out his frustration and jogged toward the parking lot, but an irregularity in the fence stopped him.

Someone had cut through the chain link then repaired the gap with zip ties.

His eyes followed the edges of the makeshift gate. It was nearly square and large enough to drive a small vehicle through. Scanning the ground outside of the fence, he traced tire tracks from a narrow dirt perimeter road, through the makeshift gate, and toward the tower he'd exited, where the tracks disappeared into the packed soil and coal.

Was this how the killer had gotten his victims onto the property?

Testing the fence, he realized some of the zip ties had been cut, creating an opening large enough for a person to get through. He squeezed through the small gap.

Fresh tracks indicated someone had parked there recently, perhaps this morning. Either the security guard had been making rounds and had stopped at this exact spot, or the killer had been nearby, watching.

Noah was too far from the others to shout his find, and he couldn't wait for them. He charged into the trees, moving up the slope at an angle as fast as he safely could, scanning the area where he'd last seen the camouflaged figure.

He pushed his way through underbrush until he was out of breath from the exertion of the climb. The light around him changed as he broke into a long narrow clearing.

No, not a clearing. It was a trail, the kind of ATV trail that crisscrossed these mountains. It had been invisible from their earlier vantage point, camouflaged by trees and—

Something hard and heavy struck his temple, robbing him of balance, of hearing, of light.

# NINE

"Noah!"

Kelsie ran, dodging roots and ruts in the ATV trail she'd followed from the parking lot. The echo of Noah's pained cry rang through the trees.

Rounding a bend, she skidded to a halt on damp leaves, barely keeping her balance.

Noah was in the center of the trail on his hands and knees, struggling to rise.

A figure stood over him, gripping a two-by-four like a baseball bat, ready to deal the fatal blow. Dressed from head to toe in hunting camouflage and wearing a matching gator that only revealed their eyes, the figure was bulky and menacing.

But those eyes weren't on Noah.

They were locked onto Kelsie.

Like a deer caught in headlights on a winding country road, the person stood frozen.

Training pushed Kelsie forward, although it felt like the world moved in slow motion. "Stop!"

Her cry seemed to panic Noah's assailant. The person tossed the board to the ground and sprinted away, rounding a bend in the trail before disappearing into the trees.

Finally, Kelsie felt as though she could move faster. She reached Noah and dropped to her knees as he dropped back to sit with his knees bent in front of him.

He waved her away. "I'm fine. Get them." Blood trickled from a gash at his hairline, and a bruise was forming on his temple. He seemed to be lucid, but he was shaky.

She looked up the trail then back to him. She couldn't leave him injured and vulnerable. What if his attacker doubled back? What if—

"Kelsie! Which way?" Footsteps pounded up the trail behind her.

Val.

Pivoting to look over her shoulder, Kelsie pointed toward the bend. "On foot. Wearing camo. Doesn't appear to be armed."

Val and Deekins sprinted past, casting glances at Noah before they disappeared in pursuit.

Kelsie turned her attention to Noah, who stared over her shoulder at nothing. While his eyes weren't glazed and the pupils seemed to be reacting normally, he could still have internal issues.

Without asking permission, she grabbed his chin with her thumb and index finger and gently turned his head so she could see the wound.

He winced but didn't protest.

The cut didn't appear to be deep, though it was

bleeding enough to look scary. Head wounds were like that. "How are you feeling?"

"Stupid." With a groan, he slowly pulled his chin from her grasp, then looked her in the eye. "I shouldn't have been charging around in the woods like a bear. Should've moved slower. He snuck up on me and rang my bell pretty good, but I think I'm okay."

She wasn't sure she believed him. "If you lost consciousness for even a second, you need to get checked out."

"I'm aware." His expression hardened. He slid back a couple of inches and moved to stand. "And I didn't."

Kelsie scrambled to her feet to help, but although he moved slowly he seemed to be steady on his feet. "You're sure you're okay?"

"I will be if you'll stop asking." He took a few deep breaths, eyeing the trees around them. "Look, he got a glancing blow. A solid one might have done me in. I didn't go all the way out, but I definitely saw some night sky stars and heard the bells ringing. Fortunately, it wasn't a 'for whom the bell tolls' kind of situation."

"You're not funny." He was a little cranky, but if he was cracking jokes, he was going to be fine.

But was she? Guilt swirled a firestorm of *what ifs* in her belly.

*What if* she hadn't walked away from him?

*What if* she hadn't come up the trail when she did? *What if* the blow had been fatal?

She had no doubt the killer had been watching from the trees as they'd searched the tower and, because she hadn't trusted her gut when she saw movement, Noah had nearly been killed. Sure, she'd voiced her suspicions, but she should have urged him to take a second look.

Instead, she'd let herself be catapulted back into a time when her heart had been his. The brief half second their eyes had locked on the stairs had rattled through her like an earthquake. Had made her sink into what used to be.

Because of her, a killer had gotten close enough to harm Noah.

This was yet another failure.

She couldn't look away as he dusted his pants and shirt, moving gingerly as though the slight movement took extraordinary effort. He was here, standing in front of her, bruised but alive, yet…

What if the killer had been successful at Noah's house? Would he have been the latest prisoner in that small, dark cell?

"Hey." Noah had stopped and she hadn't even noticed, so rapidly had her thoughts been spiraling. He leaned closer, one eyebrow raised, the trickle of blood drying on his temple. "I'm okay. Really. I'm sure Val has a first aid kit in her car. I'll get cleaned up and be fine." He twisted his lips to the side then winced as the motion pulled at his temple. "But if it makes you feel better, I'll get checked out at the ER."

Kelsie tried to pull herself together, but it was tough to look away from the man in front of her. Every ounce of her behavior today had been unprofessional. This was not who she was. She needed to be tough, sarcastic, strong... "Are you sure? Because two minutes ago you were acting like I'd have to physically drag you to—" Her voice trailed off.

*Physically drag...* The syringe... The darkness... Losing control of mind and body...

Bits and pieces of her most horrifying nightmares crashed over her like a tidal wave.

Again.

"Kels?" Noah stepped closer, steadier on his feet than he had been a moment before. "What's wrong? You turned stark white." He looked over his shoulder but, of course, saw nothing sneaking up from behind.

Because the enemy was in her mind.

"I..." *Focus, Kelsie. Focus. This is happening too often. Be an investigator. Get out of your gut and into your head. Do it.* She drew a shaky breath. "I was...thinking." She had been strong while protecting her colleague Rebecca, even when someone had tampered with Rebecca's food and nearly killed her. The incident had dragged Kelsie's worst fears to the surface.

She'd been able to combat her nightmares then.

But that hadn't been on home turf, too close to the place and the person who had ripped away her future...

Whoever he was.

He had no name, no face, no identity. He was a shadow monster. A harsh whisper. A terror.

A shudder rattled her teeth, and she clenched her jaw.

She could do this. She had to. Noah's life depended on it.

"What were you thinking?" He started walking down the trail, moving slowly until she caught up.

She should have thought of getting him off the trail and into a safe place sooner. Her brain was a mess.

"Kelsie? Thinking what? Something about this case?"

"Yes." She forced her feet into motion and tried to ground herself in the cold air, the sound of the breeze high in the trees, and the milky light filtering through the clouds. "We had to climb up those stairs. I'm in good shape, and it still took some effort. There's basically no way someone carried another human being up, especially if they were unconscious dead weight. The victims had to have walked up under their own power. Either the killer threatened them, promised them something when they reached the top—"

"Or he drugged them into submission." Noah's

voice was low. "The syringes point in that direction."

She stopped walking. Something in his voice was off, like he was thinking about more than the case. Before he could take another step, she caught up and blocked his path, scanning his face. "Are you really okay?"

"I'm good." He moved around her and kept walking.

He seemed fine, but was he? What if he had a concussion? Or he dropped with a brain bleed?

Then she'd have missed her final chance to save him.

Like he'd missed the chance to save her.

The truth hit her heart like a sniper's bullet.

For sixteen years she'd laid blame at his feet for not protecting her, for not being there when she needed him, for allowing something horrifying to happen to her. She'd raged at him, anguished over him, resented him...

And it was all because she couldn't put a face to the real perpetrator. She couldn't confront the person who had done unimaginable, irreparable harm.

Noah was no more to blame for her pain than she was for what he suffered now. He couldn't have seen the evil coming. He couldn't have known one of their friends, one of the people they both trusted, was a horrifically terrible person.

He'd thought she was safe.

And she'd never even asked him why he was late. She'd let rage and shame and bitterness fester.

She'd been wrong. The person who had drugged her, had left her broken and shamed... That man was to blame, not Noah.

"I'm sorry." The words were little more than a whisper.

Noah stopped walking and turned toward her. "What?" Confusion wrinkled his forehead, followed by a wince of pain. "What did you do?"

She opened her mouth but no sound came out. To explain would be to tell the entire story, and she could never tell the entire story. He wouldn't understand. He hadn't been there. Hadn't felt the helplessness. Hadn't felt the shame. Hadn't wondered over and over how she could have stopped it—

*Wait.*

He'd said *syringes*. Plural. More than one. Where were the others? Had—

Her phone vibrated in her hip pocket. Reflexively, she reached for it, grateful for the interruption that dragged her from her thoughts. There was too much happening at once, and her brain couldn't process it all.

She chose to focus on the incoming text.

"Kelsie? Why did you apologize?" Noah stepped closer, his expression shifting into one she'd seen before, one she'd once loved, one she would love to see again.

But there was too much between them. Too much she could never tell him.

Stepping back, she lifted the phone between them and looked at the screen, searching for control.

It was Elliott. Call me ASAP. I have news.

Noah stifled a groan as he leaned back in his desk chair and stared at the whiteboard on the wall in the field office half an hour from Hillandale. So much investigative work was done digitally now, but he'd always preferred the tactile feeling of drawing out his thoughts on a huge, clean space then watching all of the pieces fall into place.

Unfortunately, none of the pieces of his current puzzle fit together.

It was nearing seven, he was starving and his head was pounding, but he wasn't quite ready to go home. There was too much to think through.

He'd had a quick call with his parents. They were concerned about his safety, but they agreed this likely had nothing to do with their past. Still, they'd promised to be extra vigilant and to have a talk with the marshal assigned to them.

He'd also had a chat with the paramedics Kelsie had called. They'd checked him out in the parking lot of the coal prep site, but he'd declined transport to the hospital. While he'd taken a decent clock to the side of the head, he didn't think the glancing blow was anything to worry about. Aside from a nagging headache, he didn't have nausea or any other negative symptoms. Just a decent cut that, thankfully, wasn't deep enough for stitches. The blow had stunned him, but it hadn't been anywhere near fatal.

Kelsie was worried, but she'd accepted his decision in silence.

It seemed she wasn't *totally* happy with his decisions though. While he'd headed to the field office with Val, she'd turned down their invitation to brainstorm and had gone to the apartment in Hillandale.

Noah massaged his uninjured temple. If only he could figure out what was going on with her. He had no doubt he'd heard the words *I'm sorry* when they were on the trail, but he had zero idea why she'd apologized.

He also had zero idea why she repeatedly leaned in then pulled away. On the trail, there'd been yet another *zing* of what they'd once been. She'd looked as if she wanted to trust him with something…

And he'd wanted to let her. Despite the danger, he could have kissed her right there in the woods. Pulled her to him and kissed her like he used to, like he meant it, like he had when they were—

Yeah, those days were long gone, and so were those feelings, no matter how many electrical impulses his heart experienced. She'd made it clear she had no interest in him when she'd diverted her attention to her cell phone.

The woman was a riddle. Every moment they were together made him want to solve that puzzle even more than the moment before, but his head urged his heart to put on the brakes. She wasn't the Kelsie he'd loved. Something about her had changed. Sixteen years had made them both different people.

And yet—

"Hey." Val's voice came from the doorway. "Maybe you should put a pin in this until tomorrow? You've had a rough couple of days."

She wasn't wrong but, even if he went home, he wouldn't be able to sleep. "I never thought I'd be running out of fingers to count the number of personal attacks on me." It was surreal to be a victim or, well, almost a victim. He wasn't even sure how to classify himself in the reports he'd written with Val earlier. "I need to stay here and process the intel that came in. I can't figure out how any of this makes sense." Given the attacks had turned personal, it wouldn't be long before some higher-up pulled him off this case and gave it to someone else. He'd like to close it before that, or at least come as close as possible. His professional pride demanded he finish what he'd started.

She chuckled. "I figured you'd say that. Pizzas are on the way, and I had them throw in the most caffeinated drinks they had. Probably going to be a long night." Eyeballing his whiteboard, she walked over and stood near his desk. Loose hairs had straggled from her usually neat ponytail, and they hung around her face. This case was exhausting all of them. "I still think it could wait until tomorrow."

"I don't." Something about this investigation felt like they were sitting on a ticking time bomb. That feeling probably had to do with the rhythmic pounding in the side of his head. It was tough to tell if the headache had come from the way his brain had been rattled or from the riddle they desperately needed to solve.

A phone call from the medical examiner a couple of hours earlier had given them another answer, but that answer had yielded a dozen more questions.

One of the buried sets of remains had been identified. Victim number two was Ernie Hanson, a gas station clerk from a nearby small town. He'd disappeared after a night shift two years earlier. There were no witnesses and no camera footage.

At sixty-two, he'd had a fairly clean record. While he'd been accused about seven years earlier of selling alcohol to a group of underaged teens, the charges had been dropped when it was proven the kids had used fake IDs.

They'd been combing social media and cell

phone records for two hours, trying to link Ernie Hanson to their other identified victim, Jaxon Collins.

So far they'd come up empty.

Val planted her hands on her hips, scanning the information Noah had written on the whiteboard. "One recent male identified. One buried male identified. One buried male unidentified. One buried female unidentified." She looked over her shoulder at him. "If it wasn't for the female, I'd say we had someone targeting men."

"I thought of that." If the victims had all been male, then that would have at least given them a direction. But a female in the mix? That blew a lot of theories out of the water. "Have we got a profiler working this?"

"We do. I expect to hear from her tomorrow or the next day."

That was something, at least. Noah leaned back and linked his hands behind his head. He thought better of it when the move made the pounding in his temple worse. Sitting forward, he picked up a pen and tapped it on the desk. "When you throw me into the mix, everything gets more confusing. The two identified males and me...we have different ages, different backgrounds, different income brackets, different races. Other than being male, there's nothing to link us. I went through my old arrest records, and I've never crossed paths with either of them, despite the length of Collins's record."

"Due to issues with the plastic they were buried in, the remains of our unidentified male and female have more severe decomp than these first two, so we don't have solid identifying information about them."

Two identified. Two unidentified.

And him.

No two fit together.

He was too exhausted to stay upright. Leaning back in the chair, he crossed his arms over his chest this time. "Make it make sense, Yewell. I've been staring at it for so long, my eyes are crossed."

"Or maybe that's from the hit you took earlier."

He made a face, the effort tugging the cut on his head. He'd have to rely less on snarky facial expressions for a few days.

Someone pounded on the door at the front of the building.

Val glanced at her watch. "Pizza." She waved a hand for him to stay seated when he moved to stand, then walked out.

He sank into the chair and stared at the whiteboard, drawing idle circles on his desk calendar.

Sometimes it paid to look at what *didn't* fit.

He kept staring.

Yeah, that only worked if there was at least one thing that *did* fit.

*Might as well try.*

Counting himself, there were four males and one female. The female didn't fit. But since they had no ID, no age, and no identifying information, it was a dead end.

*Next.*

Neither of the identified victims were law enforcement. Given there were no missing law enforcement officers or government investigators in the area, it was likely the unidentified victims were civilians as well.

That meant he was the thing that didn't fit.

*Unless...* He pulled out a notepad. *Check for missing retired law enforcement.*

He tossed the pen to the desk and watched it roll perilously close to the edge before it bumped against an empty coffee cup.

They had nothing.

The scent of tomatoes, meat and cheese preceded Val into the room and put an end to his thought process. With a flourish, she dropped a large pizza box on the desk, then plopped a twenty-ounce soda beside it. "*Bon appétit*, Cross. Let's see if fuel will fire up the ol' brain synapses."

He said a quick blessing then flipped the box open and dug into a slice heavy with sausage and pepperoni. Not a vegetable in sight.

He was a cliché and he didn't even care.

He'd downed a full slice before he cracked

open the soda and swigged half of it. "Speed up, Yewell." He tipped the bottle toward her. "I'm a whole slice in and you're only halfway through your first."

She laughed and pointed at the pizza. "Actually, this is my second. You weren't paying attention." Taking a hefty bite, she chewed then swallowed. "The Navy taught me to cram food in quick."

"I guess." He polished off another piece before he spoke again. Grabbing a third slice, Liam walked to the board and stared at it. "I have thoughts."

"Fire away." Val took another bite of pizza.

"Okay, let's look at this from the angle—" The board swam in front of him. Noah wobbled, then righted himself as the wave of vertigo passed. He cleared his throat. "So, let's look at this from—" The room tilted.

Noah reached for the board to steady himself. He planted his feet wider as a wave of nausea rolled in.

Something was wrong.

The slice of pizza slipped from his fingers. Why weren't they working? What was happening?

Val was at his side, her grip tight on his elbow. "Cross, talk to me."

He tried to look at her, but his vision swam with the movement. Words banged against each other in his skull, but they couldn't seem to break into the air. "I'm…" His breath shook. His skin sheened with sweat. "Maybe… Head…" His knees gave out, and he crumpled.

The room whirled, tilted…

And vanished.

# TEN

Okay, Val had been right.

Kelsie polished off the last of the macaroni and cheese and teriyaki chicken then scraped the edges of the bowl with her fork, seeking every last drop of delicious. It was an odd combination, but it was perfection. The noodle shop across from her rental was right on the money.

She leaned against the kitchen counter, still holding the black plastic takeout container. Her first good, solid meal in what felt like forever had restored her mind and her mood.

Holding the container at eye level, she considered running her finger around the inside to pick up anything her fork had missed, but then she thought better of it. She wasn't two years old, after all.

Or maybe she was.

She swiped a drop of teriyaki sauce then dumped the trash before settling onto the couch with her sock feet on the coffee table. After glancing at her phone, she tossed it to the cushion beside her.

Still no return call from Elliott. He'd sent her straight to voicemail earlier, so she'd tried to call fellow investigator Gavin Mercer, even though he was on vacation. Of course, he hadn't answered.

She'd considered calling Rebecca or Hayden, but with newborns in both of their houses, she'd held off in case everyone was catching some much-needed shuteye.

She closed her eyes. Since she'd eaten, there was nothing to distract her from thinking.

Her thoughts didn't run to curiosity about Elliott's text, although that should *probably* be her focus. And they didn't turn to the Trenton Daniels case either, although that should *definitely* be her focus. It was the whole reason she was sitting here like a bundle of nerves in Hillandale instead of chilling at her own house in Carolina.

No, her thoughts ran straight to Noah.

Maybe they'd run to him for longer than she cared to admit. If she was honest, she'd never fully put him out of her mind. Although she'd refrained from googling his name until the day she took this assignment, there was still some part of her mind that drifted to him daily. A snippet of a song or a line on a television show popped into her memories at the worst moments.

She always shoved him into the far reaches of her mind, refusing to acknowledge the years of good times they'd had and the love they'd shared. It hurt too much to think of what might have been if that night had never happened.

How different would life look if Noah had been there tossing bean bags at cornhole beside her? Sharing a plate of food? Sharing a red plastic cup of syrupy sweet tea?

Which of those things had been her downfall?

She opened her eyes and stared at a crack in the ceiling.

How different would Noah's life look if she'd caught the killer in Burke's Garden on day one? If she'd seen the ATV sooner? If she hadn't left him to trail the bad guy alone today?

She pressed her palms against her eyes. Colors whirled beneath the pressure, dancing in swirls of light and darkness.

She allowed her mind to wander through memories she never visited. For a couple of years after she dropped out of college and joined the army, she'd locked herself behind dead-bolted doors and downed a few drinks to shut them down, but the feeling of being out of control never sat well.

It always panicked her more.

And what if she'd stayed in school? Hadn't stopped dancing? Had continued to don the pink slippers and the tutus and—

*Beautiful ballerina.*

She nearly gagged. Never again. Never again

would she be what that harsh, ugly whisper had quietly called her, had pursued her for being.

Rocketing to her feet, she paced the room. She would not fall victim to that voice the way she'd fallen victim to—

She inhaled deeply, all the way into her core. She paced. And paced. And paced.

If Noah had been there, she'd have continued to pursue ballet. She'd have worn her toes to nubs and—

And what? Become a principal dancer the way her mother had dreamed?

Would she have even been good enough to twirl in the background?

Would that have been enough for her mother?

Kelsie had been a phenom in the Virginia hill country, had even been accomplished enough to attend the Ailey School. But given how quickly she'd fallen apart, chased by that whisper, would she have had the strength it'd take to achieve her mother's dreams?

That night had violently altered the course of her life, but had it destroyed a dream that wasn't even hers?

That night, she'd walked away from her hometown, from Noah and from God.

But what if…

She sank onto the edge of the couch, a new thought drifting through her. What if that redirection had been right?

Oh, there was no doubt what had happened to her had been wrong. Terribly wrong. The thin few memories she could recall brought nausea and panic.

But the results...

*But God.*

She uttered the name she'd abandoned long ago. But had He abandoned her?

*What if...*

Kelsie scrambled up, her heart racing. It had been bad. It had been awful. It had been a living, nightmarish hell on earth.

But what if...what if good came from evil? What if the horrors could be flipped and used for—

Wasn't there a verse? It had been so long since she'd picked up a Bible or memorized Scripture but... Joseph had told his brothers that what they'd meant for evil, by faking his death and selling him into slavery, God had used for good to place him in a position of power that allowed him to rescue their people from a famine.

*Could it be possible?*

Her mind raced. Her breaths were panicked gasps.

It was too much to consider. Too much.

She grabbed her phone and punched a contact, mentally apologizing as she did.

Rebecca Campbell Adler answered on the first ring. "Tell me you're calling to offer me an all-expenses-paid vacation to a resort where I can sleep for ten weeks. If you're not, then don't bother speaking."

At the sound of her one true friend's voice, the panic ebbed. She was able to grab a deep, solid breath.

Kelsie sat on the edge of the coffee table, gripping the phone. It took a moment for her vocal cords to relax. "You can come and work this case that's turning itself inside out as we speak."

Rebecca chuckled. "I'll pass. Round-the-clock baby feedings require less brain power."

"How's the little girly-girl doing?" Rebecca and her husband, Heath, had welcomed little Allison into the world five weeks before. Named after Rebecca's sister, who'd been murdered the prior year, Allison was the most precious thing Kelsie had ever seen. While she'd long ago given up on children of her own, she'd never minded chilling out with someone else's for a few minutes...at least until they spit up or threw a tantrum.

"She's good. Other than thinking awake time is any time she determines, she's a perfect little girl."

"And Liam?" Rebecca had been granted guardianship of her young nephew upon her sister's death. Now nearly two, Liam had joyfully welcomed his little sister.

At first.

"He's a little clingy, a little tantrum-prone, but he's coming out of it. Heath has been great with him." Rebecca sighed. "But you didn't call to talk about my family. You probably called because you can't get ahold of Elliott after that text he blew up our phones with."

She really didn't know why she'd called, but that seemed like a valid excuse. "It's concerning when he does that then vanishes."

"No kidding." The rustling over the line said Rebecca was settling in to talk, probably on the sofa in her living room.

That room was as clear in Kelsie's mind as her own home. They'd sat there with pizza and fizzy water on the night Rebecca had figured out she was still in love with Heath and had raced out the door to tell him so. Kelsie had finished up her pizza and spent the better part of an hour watching little Liam sleep, experiencing post-trauma peace like she'd never felt before.

Rebecca clearly swigged her drink, probably that disgusting fizzy water, before she started the story. "Elliott is in a meeting with the SBI. Apparently, Quinton Pierce, the prisoner who keeps toying with us about giving out information, dropped that there might be a witness in protective custody who knows something."

"What?" Kelsie was on her feet, pacing to the French doors overlooking the parking lot. "Somebody out there might have answers?" She prayed, genuinely and fully prayed, it was so.

Their teammate Hayden McGrath and his wife,

Mia, had lost so much at the hands of a killer. Mia's first husband, Keith, had been Hayden's best friend. Several years before, he'd been murdered in what appeared to be an armed robbery gone south. As deputies at the time, Mia and Hayden had been the first to arrive on the scene, and the tragedy had scarred them both. It had taken them time to heal, but they'd found love with one another.

The wound had opened again when new evidence suggested Keith's death might not have been accidental. State investigators suspected there was an organized crime ring operating in eastern North Carolina, and the killer's behavior indicated he might have been waiting for Keith to arrive on the scene.

It might have been a hit.

But why?

Casting aside her own fears, Kelsie stared into the evening darkness. "Beck?" The silence was dragging on for too long.

"Sorry. I'm on mom brain and no sleep." Rebecca's light voice sobered. "Quinton claims he doesn't know who the protected witness is, but that he's heard rumors."

"Do *we* know who?"

"Not yet."

"But someone out there knows something?"

"Yes, and there's more. Last time Elliott called, he said…" Rebecca sniffed and steadied her voice as though emotions were getting the best of her. "According to Quinton, Keith was being surveilled, but he won't say by who. All he's let out is someone was watching the house and his movements for a while. They knew he liked to hit that particular convenience store when he needed something late at night, and when he rolled out with baby Ruthie in tow—"

"They set a plan into motion." Pulling a chair from the small dining table, Kelsie sank into it. "Which is worse, losing your husband to a random killing or knowing he was targeted?"

"They're both awful, but the second option raises a lot of questions. And it drags out the investigation and the grief for Mia and Hayden and even Ruthie."

"Worse, it calls into question how truly safe Mia and Ruthie are, if Keith was a target." The pair had already been threatened by someone not involved with Keith's death. How would their family handle the fact that danger might still be lurking? "Can we even get into contact with a protected witness? How does—"

Her phone beeped, and she glanced at the screen.

*Val.*

She'd ignore it, but given Noah's head injury, it was better to see what was up. "Let me call you back, Beck. I need to take this."

"I'm racking out here in a bit and hoping for a

solid two hours, so call tomorrow. Or I'll call you if Elliott reaches out."

"Sounds good. Sleep well." Kelsie pressed the button to switch calls. "Val? What's—"

"Meet me at the hospital." Val's voice was rushed and frantic, driving Kelsie to her feet. "Someone poisoned Noah."

"In the grand scheme of things, this could have been a whole lot worse."

Noah sank onto his couch and looked up at his partner, who stood near the door being her usual pragmatic self. "With all due respect, Val, it doesn't feel like it." The room wavered, his head pounded, and if his stomach didn't stage a revolt in the next sixty seconds, he'd count it as one of the greatest blessings of his life.

Val was right, though, even if he wasn't ready to admit it out loud. This truly could have been much worse.

He could have been dead.

Field tests indicated someone had intercepted their drinks between the restaurant and the office, then had inserted a needle into the plastic bottles. Both his cola and Val's peach tea tested positive for high doses of Rohypnol.

Their saving grace was Val hadn't opened her bottle before he succumbed.

Val said the delivery driver seemed to be an average young woman, and they were in touch with the pizza place to get a statement from her, but still...

How had someone gotten to their drinks? And if the end game was to kidnap then kill, why poison him when Val was right there? Why bring enough Rohypnol to his house to wipe him out of existence? Had that been a dosage error? But why come at him on the back of an ATV?

Nothing made sense. It was as though something about him had thrown the killer off their game.

Including the woman standing at the end of his sofa.

Kelsie waited nearby as though she wasn't sure she was welcome. Her face was stark white, her ponytail was in danger of completely escaping the band she'd roped around it and her hands were shaking. If he didn't know better, he'd think she'd ingested Rohypnol right alongside him.

*Rohypnol. Again.*

"I'll get you some water." Kelsie headed for the kitchen, clearly unsure what her function in the house was.

Val didn't move from her position by the front door, though her gaze followed Kelsie's retreat before it swung back to Noah. "I think you taking tomorrow off is a good idea."

He didn't. Clearly, he was a target, so the sooner they took down whoever was doing this, the better off he would be, and the safer the community would be. "We'll see how I feel in the morning. We're running seconds off the clock." His words slurred and his thoughts seemed to suffer from low bandwidth, but he knew what he wanted to say. "If this is related to our serial killer, then they're changing their MO. It appears there were months, maybe years, between victims before. Not this time."

"Well, you pushing too hard and landing in the hospital or worse isn't going to do anybody any favors."

"I know my limits."

Kelsie's nervous laugh preceded her into the living room. "That has literally never been true."

He'd turn his head to glare at her, but the motion was certain to set the room onto a tilt-a-whirl. Give him a second and—

She walked over carrying a travel cup and a straw. She sat it on the end table beside him, ignoring the withering look he fired at her. "You won't have to tilt your head to drink this way, so it will save you from a bumpy ride when you're ready for some water." She shoved her hands into the back pockets of her jeans, jutting her elbows out to the side. "What else do you need?"

"I'm fine." He let his eyes slide past her to Val, who hadn't moved, but he didn't turn his head. "You can both go home."

"No." If the two women had spent days rehearsing their response, they couldn't have been more perfectly in sync.

*"With all due respect, Noah,"* Val mocked his earlier statement, "not only are you coming down off the Rohypnol, but you've been targeted, what, four times? Pretty sure you aren't in any condition to defend yourself if trouble comes calling tonight."

"You shouldn't even be here." Kelsie looked down at him. "If your attacker comes back, they know exactly where you live."

"I own a gun and I'm trained to use it." If only he could aim straight.

It was probably best to keep quiet about his spinning vision.

Not only did he feel like the garbage inside of the truck that had hit him, he was dealing with two women who wanted to treat him like a toddler who was fascinated by that same garbage truck. "You can leave."

"No can do." Val crossed her arms over her chest. "One of us is staying. We can decide, or you can decide."

"No." Turning away from Val, Kelsie locked her gaze with his. "I'll stay."

A long moment passed while their eyes held, and something waved through him that had nothing to do with the Rohypnol trying to process out of his system—though the drug definitely wasn't helping him grab onto whatever feeling pulsed in his chest.

All he knew for certain was it happened every time she looked him in the eye, and that was happening more and more as the day wore on.

Kelsie broke the moment and looked over her shoulder at Val. "I've got this."

"Sounds like a plan." Val didn't seem bothered by Kelsie taking charge. "Want me to run and get you anything?"

"No." Stepping around the coffee table, Kelsie put herself between Noah and Val. "I think we're all good. What he really needs is to sleep it off and to drink plenty of liquids."

Interesting that Kelsie was so confrontational and possessive so suddenly. It might be amusing in any other circumstance.

His mind was quickly giving up its capacity to consider why Kelsie was behaving this way though. All he knew was she was right. He wanted water and sleep.

After a quiet conversation near the door, Val left and Kelsie quietly wandered the house, shutting down lights and checking the security of his doors and windows. There was an urgency to her movements that overwhelmed the usual slow grace she glided through life with.

This thing was taking a toll on them all.

She reappeared in the den while he was trying to decide if he had the energy to make it all the way up the hall to his bed. "You don't have an alarm on the house?"

"Not yet." It should have been the first thing he'd done, but he'd been a little lazy, if he was being honest. What guy imagines he's going to be in in the crosshairs of a serial killer? "Hey, thanks for staying. I keep clean sheets on the guest bed, towels in the bathroom, blankets in the hall closet." Good thing his mom had taught him hospitality, even if he wasn't the greatest at showing it from his planted spot on the couch.

He yawned, and even that slight motion made his head rock. "I think I'll stay here sitting straight up and not moving." Between the nausea, the dizziness and the anxiety that pumped through his veins with every heartbeat, there likely wouldn't be much sleep tonight. He'd read about the effects of Rohypnol, but living through them was a whole different animal.

Kelsie's expression didn't change. "If you lie down and prop up, you'll sleep better. The rocking will get worse for a second, but it will eventually stop. I'll grab a blanket out of the closet." She disappeared up the hall.

How did she know so much? Then again, she'd been a military police officer. Likely, they'd trained on the effects of multiple drugs.

But he'd trained, too, and he'd had no practical knowledge the way she seemed to.

He'd ask, but she'd never answer.

And he had a more important question anyway. When she reappeared with a blanket and the pillow from his bed, he was ready. "Kels, what made you stay here?"

She froze, the blanket hovering over the couch as though she couldn't seem to release it. She cleared her throat. "Now or for the investigation?"

Both, actually, but one was more important than the other. "Now."

Her jaw shifted to the side. "I feel like I've fail—" She laid the pillow and blanket beside him then walked to the front door, checking the dead bolt for a second time. She didn't turn around when she spoke. "How well do you know Val?"

"We've worked together for several months. She's a squared-away agent, knows her stuff, very good at observation." He was rambling. It was tough to wrestle his words into submission. "Why?"

"No reason." She shrugged. "Are you okay if I hang out in the guest room? I have a feeling if I stay in here, you're going to try to play host instead of sleeping this thing off."

She wasn't wrong.

He nodded, and she left the room.

He watched her go. Whatever her questions about Val had been, they certainly weren't *nothing*.

He wasn't sure he wanted to pursue answers that might lead him to a whole lot of *something*.

# ELEVEN

These nights of broken sleep were no longer going to cut it.

Kelsie glanced at her watch and fluffed the pillows. She'd been sitting on top of the comforter, still wearing the sweater and jeans it felt like she'd donned days earlier, dozing on and off. Her thoughts were twisted up with her past, with Noah and with creeping suspicions about Val Yewell.

She really needed her full wits about her for that one, and sleep would help.

If only she could doze off.

Deep sleep, unconsciousness, loss of control in any way terrified her to the point her body refused to rest. Every few minutes, she walked to the head of the hallway to peek at Noah in the muted light that filtered into the den from over the stove in the kitchen.

He seemed to be resting relatively peacefully.

Such a difference from the night she'd had her dad pick her up, dizzy and certain she was dying, sick with the knowledge of what had happened to her, even though she couldn't remember a thing.

Nothing but waking up in darkness, that harsh whisper still grating in the air of the barn's storage room. *Beautiful ballerina.*

Her father had accused her of drinking. She'd let him believe it. She couldn't tell him what had happened, how she was not okay, how she was not—

She shuddered and tried to shake it off, but the memories kept crashing in.

Sleep had never come. She'd lain on her bed, curled in a ball, drifting in and out of semiconsciousness. Terrified, shaking and nauseated from the drug in her system and the knowledge horrible things had happened to her. Things she both wanted to and dreaded to remember. Things she'd never told—

A new sound came from the living room. Movement. Rustling.

She was on her feet and up the hallway in an instant. She padded her way to the corner and listened.

It was Noah. Tossing. Turning. His breaths were stuttered and quick.

Kelsie's heart ached. The physical and psychological anxiety from the drug coupled with the violation was the worst.

Creeping across the semidark living room, she sat on the coffee table and reached for his hand when he swung it through the air, fighting nightmares. Gently, she wrapped her fingers around his and leaned in. "It's Kelsie. You're safe."

He awoke with a gasp and jerked his hand away, scrambling to sit upright. Immediately, he dropped his head between his knees. "Bad idea."

*Bad idea* indeed. If he was sick, she'd be sick and then—

Noah sat back slowly, pressing his hands against his thighs. "I'm okay." He was breathless and, even in the dim light, it was obvious he suffered from the kind of night terror that wrung out his whole body. He dragged his hands down his face. "How long before I feel human again?"

Good question. She was still waiting sixteen years later. "Physically? You'll feel like you have the worst hangover of your life tomorrow, but then it gets better. Psychologically?" She shrugged then stood, unwilling to reveal too much. "Want some water? Gatorade?"

"No." He moved as though he was underwater, and settled with his head on the pillow.

Kelsie resisted the urge to tuck him in. He wasn't an invalid, but the drive to care for him was strong. She'd stayed to protect him, but she couldn't protect him from the monsters Rohypnol unleashed in his mind.

Only time could slay those dragons.

She turned to walk away, but his thin voice stopped her. "Kels?" When she looked down, he was watching her. "This is going to sound..." His sigh was heavy. "Could you sit with me?"

Tears pricked the backs of her eyes. Rohypnol anxiety was a double-whammy. The drug jacked up the brain while the emotional response to having been slipped something that robbed you of your mind, your body, your memories...

Now *she* might be sick.

Fighting nausea, she sat in a chair at an angle to the couch, near Noah's head.

He was silent. His breathing slowed, and the minutes stretched. It almost seemed he'd fallen asleep, but then he spoke. "How do you know so much?" The question was low, weighted and oddly intimate.

More intimate, more difficult, than he could imagine.

Knitting her fingers together, Kelsie dropped her hands into her lap. She pressed her thumbs together, letting the ache of the pressure ground her in this moment. She was safe. She wasn't semiconscious and vulnerable, at the whim of someone she'd trusted, someone who'd slipped her a substance that had allowed him to destroy her.

Somehow, Noah seemed to understand he'd asked a question more deadly than a fully loaded machine gun. He lay silently, waiting, not pushing, not forcing.

He would never push or force.

He was Noah.

Her Noah.

And that made all the difference.

Words that had been dammed up for years stirred, slicing their way through walls she'd erected long ago. She could feel them working their way up her throat, desperate for air.

Maybe it was the semidarkness. Maybe it was the earlier realization that Noah wasn't responsible for what had happened. Or maybe it was that he was lying two feet away, suffering the same physical and mental pain she'd suffered, even if their emotions and outcomes were worlds apart.

The darkness seemed to settle, but not in the way it had for years, suffocating and cold. In the quiet of Noah's living room, with his presence an arm's length away, the darkness felt like a snug blanket on a cool day, like safety and familiarity.

Like life had always felt with Noah. Safe. Secure.

Known.

Her brain couldn't comprehend how the very thing she'd feared for years was suddenly providing peace and the freedom to speak.

Although she'd wrestled back the truth for years, she actually needed to speak. "I..." The word cracked. She sniffed and started again, driven to say things she'd never said aloud to a man she'd loved and tossed. If she didn't release the words now, she'd die from suffocation. "Someone drugged me."

Noah stopped breathing. "Kels. I had no—"

"After high school." *Please don't make me say when. Please just...know.*

"After—" He inhaled sharply and sat up but dropped quickly, groaning. The nausea was quick. It was a sensation she'd never forget. "Is that why—"

It was hard to say. So hard to say. But now was the time. Noah was the person. "Yes."

The silence hung heavy. Maybe the drugs were dragging his system down and he couldn't react. Maybe he knew she needed time to work through words she was terrified of saying. They'd been sealed away for so many years they'd petrified.

*Lord, chisel them out. Set me free.*

Set her free? Since when did she believe God listened, let alone answered? He'd allowed her to suffer. How was He good? How was He trustworthy?

And yet...

Since she was forced to face the past, it seemed she was forced to face Him, too.

It was too much at once.

One thing a time, and the first battle was saying the words. Her spirit cried it was now or never. "I don't remember much. We were... Somebody started a cornhole tournament." The story spilled forth, the words rushing faster and faster. "I wasn't drinking. Others were. Just kicking back tea, pizza."

"That was rebellion for you." Noah's words were low, as though he feared volume might silence her.

"True." Her mother had never allowed sugar or fat. Kelsie had been trained to protect her dancer's physique at all costs. So while some kids ran for alcohol when their parents weren't looking, Kelsie ran for junk food.

If only she hadn't.

Not that it would have mattered. Any food, any drink was a target. "Last thing I remember is... I got dizzy, nauseated out of nowhere." Her voice cracked. Maybe the words didn't want to be free after all. They lodged in her throat, sharp and cutting.

What came next was sheer horror.

Sheer shame.

"You walked away from the group?" Of course Noah knew. He'd been her best friend, her first love, the one who knew the way her mother had trained her, had brought her up to be strong, to be perfect, to never be a bother to anyone at any time.

"The barn was right there." If only she'd been taught differently, taught to ask for help instead of hiding her weaknesses. She'd have never walked into the dark alone.

But she hadn't been alone.

"Noah, I don't remember anything after I walked through that door into the darkness. I've tried. I've tried so hard, but there's nothing. Nothing except…" She swallowed a sob, the first time tears had threatened her in years. She cleared her throat, but the words shattered. "Somebody was there. My only memory is someone saying—" She couldn't. Those nightmare words scratched and clawed. *Beautiful ballerina*. The words had been harsh, dropped over her like a curse as he left her to spiral between consciousness and unconsciousness, sick with the truth of what had happened, of what she couldn't remember.

The words taunted her, threatening to rip her apart all over again.

Except… Tonight they were less harsh. Less loud. Less forceful.

"Kels, did someone…" Noah's hands remained on his stomach, laced together as though he was holding himself together. "Did someone hurt you?"

She couldn't answer. Some words should never have to be spoken by anyone ever.

Her silence would speak volumes words never could.

He was Noah. He would know.

His hands on his stomach rose with one deep, long breath, as though he was absorbing the pain she'd exhaled.

What was he thinking? That it was her fault? That she shouldn't have tried to hide? That she should have known better?

Deep shame, deep fear, wormed through her veins.

"Kelsie." He breathed her name like it was reverent, so different than the ugly words twisting her thoughts. "You didn't do anything wrong."

His words roared through her, breaking like a tidal wave, drowning out the awful whisper that had ended her dancing career, because she couldn't stand for anyone to think of her as *that* ever again.

*You didn't do anything wrong.* Intellectually, she knew that, but hearing Noah speak it...

Forcing out the ugly words had left space for the truth to settle in.

Fear pulsed through her, but it was less intense, less searing.

The darkness inside of her was absorbing the light of truth that Noah spoke, that God had been waiting to speak.

Opening the valve had not only released the story—it had released the pressure. It allowed her to breathe without feeling a vise around her chest.

She dropped her chin, and her first tear in years broke free. It tracked an agonizingly slow path down her cheek. Another followed, but she swallowed the rest, refusing to give in to the sobs that would rack her if she truly let go.

She was freer, but she wasn't ready for that. Not yet.

Not when Noah needed her as much as…

As she needed him.

She needed a minute. The new sensations, the new light, were overwhelming. The truth was agonizing. She needed time.

And Noah needed rest. She stood. "If you need me, I'm here."

She could barely make out his face in the shadows. "Same." His voice was shaky.

Was it because of what had happened to him? Or what had happened to her?

She turned to leave, but his whisper stopped her. "Don't go."

Did he need her? Or did she need him?

Did it matter?

She looked down. Their gazes locked and held, drawing her in. She eased to the floor. Pulling his hand from his stomach, she twined her fingers with his, rested her head on the couch, and held on…for both of them.

Noah tightened his grip on her hand, wishing he never had to let go.

It was his fault she had endured so much pain, that her life had completely derailed.

Guilt and grief and residual drugs rocked him with nausea so intense it threatened to stop his heart. He needed her beside him to get him through, but she needed him just as much.

He'd failed her once. Big-time.

It was his fault for not being there. His fault for trying to fix that stupid truck instead of borrowing his dad's car and going straight to her on their last night together.

If only he'd done things differently. If only he'd...been there.

It was clear she didn't know who the perpetrator was, but given who was at the party, it had to be someone she'd known, someone she'd trusted.

Someone *he'd* known and trusted.

Anger mixed into the toxic blend already coursing through his system. Who would harm Kelsie? Who would steal—

Beside him, her breaths came short and quick, as though she was still dealing with the fallout.

Surely she was. It was in her refusal to eat food he offered to bring to her. Her refusal to let him drive. Everything was about control, about preventing the worst from happening again.

"I am so sorry." It would be amazing if she heard the words his heart cried. He was supposed to love and protect her, and he'd failed.

"Noah." She lifted her head from the cushion, and his name brushed his cheek. "You couldn't have known."

Didn't she understand? It didn't matter. He should have been there. "But—"

"Up until, well, today... I blamed you. I was so angry with you." Her words were quiet, but breathed so close to his ear, they carried weight.

He could feel them. "I blamed you for not being beside me, for abandoning me, for not stopping it. But Noah… You couldn't have. If someone was determined…" She inhaled a shaky breath. "I've been with you twice today and couldn't protect you. Over and over the past couple of days, you've nearly died, at times right in front of me, and I couldn't stop it. You couldn't stop it." She rose on her knees, her grip on his hand tightening as though she could force him to understand. "You aren't…him."

She was right, but it would take a long time and a lot of prayer before he could slake the fire of guilt that threatened to burn him to ashes from the inside out. "And it's not you. You're not to blame."

"Maybe."

"Definitely." It cost every ounce of strength and balance he had to sit up against the pillow. He had to catch his breath and give his inner ear a minute to stop the room from tilting before he could speak. "Someone did something terrible to you, and he's at fault." She'd carried unthinkable pain for years, had suffered as no one ever should at the hands of…

Of who? He assumed based on her wording that she didn't know, but he hadn't asked. "Who was it?" He was ready to fight, ready to defend. His anger was as real as both of their pain.

"I don't know." She seemed to shrink. "I knew everybody there, and there was no one I didn't trust at some level or another, nobody I would think would do something so…terrible. I don't remember."

She was holding something back, but it wasn't the person's identity. There was more to her story, things she'd likely never tell anyone. He'd seen it before with victims of violence. Some things were too difficult, too horrible, to ever speak out loud.

Oh, how he wished he could take away her pain. He wanted so badly to extract his hand from her grasp and to touch her, but that likely wasn't something she'd welcome, given the memories she'd shared. "It wasn't your fault."

"I shouldn't have walked away by myself. I should have told someone. I should have asked for help." The words poured forth. She pulled her fingers from his, anguish coating her declarations.

"And he'd have been the one to pretend to rescue you." Whoever it was, he'd have made certain to be in prime position to strike. But there was another person at fault as well. "Your mother raised you to always be the epitome of grace and quiet and propriety. She didn't do you any favors by teaching you negative emotions are bad and needing help is the same as causing trouble." He'd been a kid back then, one who'd had no idea how to confront an adult about their ugly behavior, but he'd always known the way Kelsie's mother talked to her, berated her, insisted on perfection from her was damaging. It was a wonder Kelsie hadn't full-on rebelled against the strain.

As it was, she'd guzzled soda and candy whenever she was away from home, laughed loudly and slouched in her chair whenever possible, just to "feel human," she'd once confessed.

"I still walked away." Pain and regret hung in the air between them.

"You didn't drug yourself."

"I know." She dropped back to sit, resting her head on the sofa. Her hair brushed his cheek. "When I was an MP, I saw so many women who blamed themselves or let someone else blame them. I knew they shouldn't. I knew *I* shouldn't. But... I needed to hear someone say it...to me." She reached for his hand, but this time, her touch was different, not the desperate grasp of someone trying to calm his anxiety. This was the gentle grasp of someone reaching out to share with a friend.

Or...maybe more?

If he could shake the thought out of his head without losing his lunch, he would. The last thing Kelsie needed was for him to try to rekindle old feelings.

Their time had passed, hadn't it?

He was pretty sure a flame had fanned to life the moment he'd seen her in Burke's Garden. What should he do with it? She'd wrap up her case soon, then she'd be gone. Was he ready for her to walk out of his life one more time, for good?

Oblivious to his thoughts racing in a whole new direction, she settled beside him as though she was reluctant to leave.

Something rested between them, something both old and new.

He wasn't sure what to do with it, but he definitely didn't want it to end.

# TWELVE

"How's the patient?" Rebecca's voice over the cell sounded like the baby might have finally let her get some sleep.

Kelsie looked over her shoulder at Noah's kitchen door and stepped off the patio into his yard. The woods stood close around the house, sheltering it from the cold wind that bent the treetops. The clouds that had threatened snow for days had dissipated, leaving a brittle blue sky above.

That was fine by her. Winter roads in the mountains were one of her least favorite things.

She sipped the cup of coffee she'd brewed and checked again to make sure Noah hadn't come outside. "He's fine. It took him all day yesterday to fully detox, so he was pretty miserable. This morning he said he was finally feeling like himself."

Two nights ago, she'd fallen asleep with her head resting by Noah's on the couch. When she'd awakened yesterday morning, she'd been shocked to see the sun filtering into the living room.

While her back had ached in a way that reminded her she was no longer a young woman, her heart and mind had felt lighter. She'd slept soundly and deeply the entire night for the first time in years. No waking at every sound. No sleep-stealing fear she'd be caught helpless. No nightmares, no dreams, no memories of hideous whispers in the dark. Just sleep that had let her awaken feeling rested and new.

Just safety. Just peace.

She'd taken some of the power from her fears by speaking the truth.

Or maybe it was because... Well, because Noah had been close by.

She wasn't ready to ask herself how she felt about that.

"Did you stay there this whole time? Two nights?" Rebecca's question spun forth slowly, tinted with incredulity.

Her surprise wasn't unearned. The whole team knew Kelsie rarely, if ever, slept if other people were nearby. They assumed she'd trained herself to be hypervigilant.

They had no idea there was so much more to it.

"I did. Noah was pretty unsteady yesterday, and it was a fight to get him to take the day off. I finally talked him into taking it easy by combing through the old case files on Daniels and then looking back over the evidence in these newly uncovered homicides. Besides the burial site, there's zero evidence to connect the two cases, so there's little chance of the defense being able to use this to bolster their request for a retrial. I talked to Elliott and we're moving forward on the Daniels relook." The state had extended the deadline for Trinity to report their findings and had also hired the team to stay on and consult with the current investigation since Kelsie was familiar with the particulars. "Elliott is arriving this afternoon to work on both cases with us." He'd had little more to offer on his cryptic text, just that Quinton Pierce was releasing information very slowly from his prison cell and there had been no new intel on the protected witness, who may or may not actually exist.

"He told me. Have you guys heard anything back about the evidence from the coal plant?"

"Nothing yet. We're still waiting on prints, and the area had been scrubbed down pretty well. The state is working on getting records from satellite internet companies and from cell phone towers to see if anything pops."

"That would give you some answers." Rebecca's voice shifted and filled with amusement. "But hey, you know I have a thousand other questions totally unrelated to this case but that have everything to do with a certain investigator *on* the case."

"And you know I won't answer them." Not right now. Not when she wasn't sure what was happening in her own heart and mind. She'd not slept in the same room with anyone, male or female, since her military days, which had been racked by raging insomnia she'd never admitted to anyone for fear of being chaptered out.

"Interesting. I seem to remember you charging onto my front porch a while back, insisting I dump my entire history with Heath at your feet. That was you, wasn't it? Brunette ponytail, supreme nosiness, lethal ninja moves?"

True, she had stuck her nose all up in Rebecca's business concerning her ex...the man she'd eventually married.

They didn't need to go any further with this conversation if Rebecca was going to ring wedding bells for Kelsie and Noah.

Besides, this call was about something more. Something that might be bigger. "I need to run a few thoughts by you. I want an unbiased opinion."

"This sounds serious." Rebecca's teasing tone vanished. "Both kids are asleep, shockingly, so you have my undivided attention."

"Good, because this is kind of big." Something had been eating at her and, although she'd hinted it to Noah, she wasn't sure he'd caught on. Given the drugs in his system when she'd mentioned it, he might not even remember the conversation.

Kelsie looked at the back door again then walked deeper into the yard, scanning the shadows, very aware a killer knew exactly where Noah lived. "It's about Special Agent Val Yewell. She works in the field office with Noah, and I've got some thoughts."

"Let's hear them."

Kelsie laid out the series of incidents targeting Noah. "He was attacked at home, and Val knows where he lives. He was attacked in Bramwell, and Val knew where he was. He was attacked on that trail, and Val was not in sight until it was over. And she was present and handled his food last night. Her drink was tainted, too, yet she never took a sip."

"You know, I feel a kinship with Noah right about now." Rebecca knew what it was like to be stalked and drugged by someone she trusted.

Maybe Kelsie should have talked to her about her own experience long before now. Maybe this new lightness in her body and spirit could have come sooner. How much had she sacrificed by holding it all in and trying to be strong on her own? How many friends had she alienated?

"I'll say this from the jump, after hearing your suspicions." Rebecca's voice was slow, thoughtful. "A couple of the incidents would have required her to be in two places at once, especially the one on the trail at the coal facility. There, she was in the parking lot with the security guard when the attack happened."

She'd thought of that. "Maybe there's an accomplice?"

"Possibly. If you really wanted to stretch, you

could look into that security guard, Deekins, who had access to the processing plant and who Val paired up with when you guys investigated. But what's the motive? She works with Noah, but has he mentioned any beef? Why come at him now? And what about the other victims? What would be her motive for killing them? You seem pretty certain the person in Burke's Garden is the same person coming at Noah."

"So much about all of this makes no sense." Although she'd slept well in the guest room the night before, it had taken some time to nod off. She'd awakened still spinning about whether or not Val was involved. Part of her thought *yes*, while another part said *no*. It was tough to differentiate truth from lie in so many things. "Even the known victims aren't linked in any way we can discern."

"So I'm guessing you'd like me to do an under-the-radar search on Special Agent Val Yewell?"

"Please? I don't want to open a can of worms by accusing a state investigator of murder, especially since this is really a hunch."

Behind her, the back door squeaked open. "Noah's coming. I have to go, but I'll be in touch." She killed the call and pocketed her phone before she turned.

Noah carefully made his way down the two steps to the patio, watching Kelsie. He'd spent yesterday in sweats and a T-shirt, creeping gingerly around the house as though the slightest quick movement would topple him. He'd confessed to brain fog and lingering nausea, but he'd awakened this morning ready for breakfast, coffee and work.

Seeing him walk outside in dark dress slacks, a white button-down shirt and his dark coat was jarring after the casualness of the previous day. Sixteen years had only served to make him more attractive, to chisel his soft teenaged edges into maturity. She hadn't let herself notice before, but since she'd laid the truth out before him, it was as though her eyes could see more clearly.

Any woman would be foolish not to like what she saw.

But it was what she couldn't see, what lay beneath the surface. Noah was kind, considerate, open... He was still all of the things she'd fallen in love with years before.

And those things drew her now, even with an entire backyard between them.

The day before, they'd not discussed the past or the fact she'd slept on the floor beside the couch. Instead, they'd focused on the cases they were investigating, and then they had talked of trivial things in a way that resurrected memories of the way things used to be.

Those random conversations tugged her toward what they used to have.

If she trusted him with her story, could she trust him with more? With herself?

Back in the day, he'd been the one she talked to

about everything, big and small. There had been no secrets between them. Now, once again, he was the one she'd run to, even after years of shutting him out and blaming him.

He was still her safe place.

The truth rocked her so hard she took a step back.

*Noah? Her safe place?*

Did that mean... If she could trust Noah, did she dare trust the God she'd begun to reflexively cry out to again?

Noah approached, his eyebrow arched in question. "Are you okay?"

*Oh my word.* This was too much all at once.

*He* was too much all at once. Oh yes, her eyes had been opened and she could see him...really see him.

She could feel him...really feel him.

And he was...everything.

Turning her back to him, she took a long draught of coffee that was still too hot. Blinking back tears, she let the scald in her throat ease to a low burn before she spoke. "I'm fine."

"Good, because Val called. They've identified another set of remains from Burke's Garden."

Well, this was good news. Slinging the rest of her coffee into the bushes, she squared her shoulders and faced him. They matched steps as they walked back toward the house. "Does the identity of this victim give us any more answers?"

"No. It actually opens the door to a lot more questions." His voice was grim, and he stopped walking to look at her. "And, Kelsie? It's someone we know."

"Are you ready?" Noah looked at Kelsie as she navigated the curving road toward Bluefield. He'd been hesitant to bring her on this interview, especially after the truths she'd entrusted to him about that night.

"I'm fine." Her tone was clipped, and she seemed overly focused on driving.

He couldn't blame her. He was still putting together the pieces of Kelsie-before and Kelsie-after, and lightbulbs kept going off as he recognized things that explained her personality changes and choices. Every breath he took begged to exhale an apology, but she'd shut him down the last time he'd tried.

The guilt was strong.

Worse than the guilt was the tension in his heart. He was still drawn to her. She'd always been the standard and, though he'd dated over the years, no one had ever measured up. It was as though God knew she'd be back and was holding a place for her.

But it was obvious she struggled to trust, to... love. While he understood what she battled, could they have a future if she couldn't trust him? Was he willing to—

"I'm sorry." Kelsie turned onto a secondary road and flicked him a quick glance. "I wasn't expecting one of the victims to be someone we knew."

He dragged himself out of his thoughts. Frankly, he'd been as shocked as she was.

The latest identified victim was Brianna Daugherty, the mother of Will Daugherty. Will had graduated from Shiloh Peak High School two years before them, while his younger brother Drew had been eight years behind them. Will had been a quiet outdoorsy type who played football and who loved his parents' farm.

The farm where Kelsie had been attacked.

The Daugherty family had regularly opened their huge property to kids in the area. While they didn't provide refreshments, they stayed away from the weekly parties, turning a blind eye to any alcohol use.

The Daughertys had eventually divorced and sold the farm. William Senior had left town. Brianna had bought a small house in Bluefield, where the parties continued when Drew went to high school. The last time Noah had seen any of them, it had been when a young girl overdosed at Brianna's home, a tragedy that had changed them all. Though Will had stayed close, Brianna had moved away from the area.

Will now owned a massive plot of land near Bluefield, where he ran a successful horse farm.

As for Drew Daugherty, a cursory search had led to a dead end, so they were headed to talk with Will, who had been notified that morning his mother was dead. He'd read up on Brianna's disappearance, but he wanted to clarify a few things and to gauge Will's responses to a few questions, just to be sure they didn't miss anything. They'd missed the report of her disappearance, given that it had happened outside of the area, so he needed to slow down now and be extra cautious.

How would Kelsie handle coming face-to-face with someone who had been in attendance the night she was assaulted? She'd told Noah she considered everyone a suspect, and that certainly extended to Will.

Kelsie flipped on the turn signal and waited for a pickup to pass before she made the turn onto a wide packed-dirt lane. A large sign announced the home of Valley Vista Farm. She kept her eyes on the driveway. "I'll be okay. This isn't the old farm, so the memories aren't so strong."

He wasn't so sure. She'd been jumpy since he first laid eyes on her in Burke's Garden. Kelsie was strong, but could she hold it together while looking her past in the eye? Could he protect her if she fell apart?

He'd failed her once in a very big way. What if he failed her again and the emotional fallout was the last bit of weight needed to crush her?

The drive wound through pastures that waved

with the hills and valleys of the property. They passed several long barns and paddocks situated on flat land. After passing through a stand of native trees, the property opened up into a large clearing that looked along the valley to stunning mountain views.

Kelsie followed the drive as it shifted from dirt to concrete then circled in front of a large white two-story house with huge columned porches on each end. Several vehicles were parked near the house, likely family who had gathered at the news of Brianna's death.

As Kelsie shut off the SUV's engine, the front door of the house opened and a tall man stepped out. He was several inches over six feet, tanned even though it was winter, and built like someone who spent most of his time working outdoors.

The man caught Noah's eye when he exited the vehicle, then he motioned to the covered patio on the left of the house. Large outdoor heaters sat amidst several ornate metal picnic tables.

"That's Will." Kelsie hadn't needed to identify him. He'd been the tallest kid at Shiloh Peak. Despite the fact his height had made everyone assume he'd play basketball, he'd opted for football. While he hadn't been a standout, he'd been a fixture on the team, and even though they'd attended a different school, they knew who he was.

Noah looked over his shoulder at Kelsie, who hadn't moved. She read a text on her watch, then stared out the window at Will, who was making his way to the picnic tables. "You okay, Kels?"

"Go ahead. I need a minute." She stared at her hands on the steering wheel as though she wasn't sure they were attached to her body. She spoke suddenly, as though she'd had a thought. "Elliott will be here in a few hours."

That was good. A friend, her boss, someone she trusted.

Unlike him.

She certainly needed someone. The way she gripped the steering wheel, it almost seemed she feared she'd float away if she let go.

He couldn't leave her like this. He never should have brought her here. "If you want, I—

"Go." She barked the command with all of the authority she'd probably used as a military police officer.

He dared not disobey. Although every inch of him fought to sit with her as she wrestled an unjust and ugly trauma in the past, he did as she requested and left her to handle it her way...like she had for sixteen years.

Guilt chased him up the sidewalk to the covered patio where Will Daugherty stood staring at the mountains, his hands shoved into the pockets of khaki slacks. The button-down black shirt he wore was too thin to keep out the January chill that the heaters couldn't quite burn off, but he didn't seem to notice.

When Noah stepped onto the patio, Will didn't turn. "I held out hope Mom would come home. And now?" He flung his hand toward the mountains as if that explained a tragedy that defied explanation.

How many times had Noah heard the same sentiment from a victim's family? There was always hope...until hope died. "I'm sorry, Will. I wish the news had been different."

Turning, Will shook his head. His eyes were red-rimmed, and it was clear the truth was still sinking in. "I think..." He pressed his lips together and looked past Noah at nothing, his eyes sheening with tears that didn't fall. "I think knowing is better than not knowing, even when it's the worst. For too long, we've had questions, but we didn't know..." He shook his head, took a deep breath and suddenly jutted out his hand toward Noah in a polite greeting. "It's been a while, man. How've you been?"

If Noah hadn't been a Virginian himself, the switch in demeanor would have shocked him. It was such a Southern thing, to be polite in the face of adversity, to shove down emotions in order to offer hospitality. "You don't have to put up a front, Will."

Will sniffed, offered a sad smile, then sank into a chair facing the driveway. "Good. Because I don't have it in me. I've been inside all morning trying to be the man for my mom's family and friends.

I'm tired. What I really want to do is go into town and plant myself at a bar, maybe meet a woman and..." He shrugged. "Make it all go away."

"It'd still be there when you woke up in the morning." He'd never been one to drink away his problems, but the couple of times he'd tried, it had only made everything worse. As for searching for comfort in a stranger's arms? Nope. That had never been something he'd understood.

Will didn't seem to hear him, or maybe he didn't want to. "Who's your chauffeur?" He tilted his head, his eyes narrowing. "Reminds me of that ballet dancer you used to date. The ice queen."

Something visceral hit Noah at the words. *Ice queen?* Kelsie had been warm and friendly to everyone.

She didn't deserve Will's judgment or his interest. And knowing what had happened to her? She certainly wouldn't like being noticed, not when he'd been there on the night of the assault. Noah shifted to stand between Will and the SUV.

A new scent drifted toward him. So Will's red eyes weren't only from tears. The faint odor said Will had already tried unsuccessfully to drown his pain.

That was one more reason to keep Kelsie out of his line of sight. "She's a consultant."

"Lucky you." Will still tried to look past Noah, but then he shifted his gaze. "You said you had questions?"

"I do, if you're up to answering them." Noah refused to sit, not wanting to open a line of sight between Will and Kelsie again. "I hate to ask on the heels of your news this morning, but time is not our friend if we're going to find out who did this to your mother."

"Whatever you need."

*Good.* He'd ask his questions then get out quickly. He suddenly didn't feel like being around his former acquaintance any longer than necessary. "Your mother went missing two years ago in January?"

"Yeah, around the first of the year." Will slouched lower. "I'm not sure exactly when, because I was out of town on a cruise with some friends and didn't get back until the fifth. Last time I saw her was Christmas, and then she was at a party for work on New Year's Eve. She was off on New Year's Day and texted her boss on January second to say she wasn't feeling well. Nobody heard from her again."

That text wasn't worth putting a lot of faith in. It was possible the killer had already taken Brianna and was using her phone to buy time. From reading through reports about her disappearance, there'd been no forced entry, no signs of struggle. Her car had been found in the driveway and her purse and phone had been left in the house. She'd simply vanished. Much like the other two victims, there was no evidence of a crime scene, nothing in their phone records or emails to indicate trouble. They'd simply disappeared without a trace...until now.

Will dragged his hand down his face. "If you're looking for answers from me, I don't have anything more than what's already been said." He sighed. "I wish I did. Mom didn't have any enemies, no debts, nothing to get her...this."

"And what about your brother?"

"Drew?" Will's head snapped up. "You've talked to Drew?"

Something crawled along Noah's spine. "You haven't?"

"Not in over a year. He always kind of did his own thing, went his own way. He fired off a text to me on the anniversary of Mom disappearing and said he was taking his travel trailer across the country. Needed to grieve or something. Haven't heard a word out of him since."

*Hang on...* Noah flipped through the notes in his phone. Jaxon Collins, Ernie Hanson, Brianna Daugherty... Every single one of them were last seen on or around January 1.

A sick feeling swirled in the pit of his stomach.

He knew the identity of the final person in Burke's Garden, buried in a makeshift grave.

# THIRTEEN

Kelsie rubbed her temples, where a pounding headache threatened to take her out of commission. She needed more caffeine but, frankly, she was terrified to drink anything in Noah's office. While she'd relinquished some of her suspicions about Val, he'd still been hit in his office. Anything could be doctored.

Her watch buzzed. Be there in an hour.

Elliott was on the way. That was either good or bad. She hadn't yet decided which. While she'd love her boss's help, she was also dealing with so many things, she wasn't sure she needed his quiet scrutiny.

Noah dropped his phone to his desk with a clatter. He'd been talking to Val, who was with the coroner. He shifted his gaze to meet hers and shook his head, his mouth a grim line.

Her heart sank. "Are they sure?"

"Yeah." Noah dropped his gaze to his desk and spun his phone with a flick of his index finger.

"Preliminary tests indicate the final set of remains is Drew Daugherty."

Kelsie sank into the chair in the corner of Will's small office. The last time she'd seen Drew, he'd been ten years old, running around at that final party, begging to be noticed. She'd let him toss one of her throws at cornhole before he'd dashed off.

Now he was dead. It was tough to replace the image of the little boy with one of the grown man who'd been dead for a year.

*A year.* Kelsie shook off her grief for the lost little boy and looked at Noah's whiteboard. A column of dates indicated when the victims had vanished. Each missing persons report fell in the first few days of January, with the last date of contact for each being December 31 or January 1. One person every year for the past four years.

Until Noah. He'd been attacked on January 8 in the same year Jaxon Collins had. Why the difference?

She planted her elbows on her knees and stared at the floor. "What's so special about New Year's?" She looked up at another thud from Noah's desk.

He'd opened his laptop and was typing on the keyboard. "I'm not sure, but if I'm truly a potential victim, then something connects me to them, something that happened around that date."

She caught up to his thought process and hurried to stand behind him so she could see the screen. "Your old cases."

"Exactly. Something connects those four victims and me. Something we aren't seeing. I can link myself to the Daugherty family, obviously, but that's a thin thread. A lot of us were at those parties. It has to be..." His voice trailed off as he opened a database, narrowed his search by date and started scrolling. "Since I started with the BCI, there's been nothing I've worked that connects to that date."

He moved quickly, forcing her eyes to keep up as her head pounded with increasing insistence. Her body craved caffeine. "Maybe before that?" Her voice sounded thin, even to her. The words on the screen swam with the waves of an impending migraine. Stress and emotions were working against her.

Noah looked over his shoulder, bringing them nose-to-nose, then quickly turned toward the screen. "You okay?"

"Headache. Should have finished my coffee earlier instead of dumping it." She wouldn't admit she was addicted to her morning coffee, at least not out loud.

Without looking away from the screen, he grabbed his travel mug and held it over his shoulder toward her. "I filled it up with what you made at home. It's black, no creamer. It's been with me the whole time, never out of my sight except when

I was talking to Will and it was in the car with you."

She stared at the cup. On the one hand, caffeine withdrawal was real.

On the other…

Slowly, she took the cup, slid back the slider and sipped. It was still hot and, even though it was a placebo effect for sure, the effect was immediate. The headache didn't disappear, but her tension eased.

She immediately took another sip. If it had been doctored, the damage was already done.

Noah's fingers stilled on the keyboard. He seemed to stop breathing.

Leaning closer to the screen, Kelsie tried to see what had stopped him. "Did you find something?"

"What?" Shaking his head, Noah started scrolling again. "No. Just distracted."

Made sense. He'd been through a lot. She sipped the coffee again. "It it's not a case you worked with the BCI, then—"

"Then maybe…" He straightened so suddenly that the top of his head nearly connected with her chin. "Kels…" He barely said her name out loud, but it was enough.

He was on to something.

She leaned forward to see the screen better, their cheeks practically touching. She could feel him breathe.

Her eyes went out of focus, and it had nothing

to do with caffeine. It was the scent of Noah's soap. The warmth of his skin.

The fact she had accepted his coffee with little hesitation.

She'd not accepted a drink from anyone in sixteen years.

She straightened and took a step back, covering her gasp with more coffee. Her pulse raced as though she'd chugged an entire pot of the stuff.

What was she doing?

Her heart noticed him, really noticed him, in a way it hadn't at his house. She'd been so focused on caring for him, on revealing the truth, that she'd not realized the ramifications of it all.

She wasn't afraid to be near him, to touch him, to trust him. She wasn't scared he was going to suddenly turn and harm her. It went beyond that moment of confession. It was filtering into every part of her life.

This was Noah. And her heart felt—

She gripped the coffee cup with both hands. *No.* She couldn't trust her emotions. She didn't dare.

They were too fickle, and five minutes from now, she might frantically replace every brick he'd torn down. If she did, it would destroy him.

It would destroy her.

There were too many years between them. There was too much left to say. She'd hurt him when she left, had hurt him when she'd refused to contact him for sixteen years. What would it take for him to forgive her?

Too much. There was no way she could ever ask that much of him...of anyone.

Noah didn't seem to notice she'd backed away. Instead, he was intent on reading the screen. "I've got something."

Kelsie stepped around the desk, nursing the coffee while he silently ready, his expression growing more steely with each passing moment.

When he finally sat back and dragged his hands down his face, he looked haggard and worn, as though he was still wrestling with the physical effects of the Rohypnol. "Seven years ago, I was among the first on scene when a young woman died at a party. Corinna Phillips. It was a drug overdose."

Her eyes slipped shut. She knew where part of this was going. "The party was at Will's."

"Close. I should have connected the dots sooner, but it didn't click because it wasn't at the farm. It was at Brianna's new house, back when Drew was in high school."

"Oh, boy." Kelsie stared at the whiteboard, pieces clicking into place to create a terrible, twisted, vengeful image. She traced her finger along the cool, smooth surface of the board, connecting the dots. "A girl dies. Brianna green-lighted the party, or at least turned a blind eye to it. She's murdered. Drew threw the party. He's murdered." She dragged her finger to another name. "Jaxon Collins?"

"Was busted for selling drugs to some kids that were there."

"So he possibly sold the drugs that killed the girl. For the moment, we can assume so." She shifted to the next name. "Ernie Hanson?"

"I was new to the unit and was tasked with the grunt work, but I did talk to Will and interviewed most of the kids at the party. I wasn't involved in the rest of the case or I'd have picked it up sooner, but some of the kids indicated they'd bought alcohol even though they were underaged. They got it from—"

"Ernie Hanson."

"Yeah." Sitting forward, Noah clicked the mouse and moved to something else. "That party got him busted for selling to minors."

"So..." Kelsie straightened, her headache forgotten and her own problems fading. This was her wheelhouse...investigating, digging, setting everything where it belonged. "So a girl dies at a party seven years ago. Three years later, someone starts to systematically take out everyone they feel is responsible. The owner of the house, who's an adult and should have protected the kids instead of standing idly by. The person who threw the party. The person who provided the alcohol that likely escalated the chaos. The dealer who provided the drugs that may have killed the girl." Her voice slowed, and she looked over her shoulder at Noah, who was watching her work. "And you?"

"If they came after Drew, then it's likely they were at the party and saw me interview him. Honestly, he was pretty upset, and I took him aside to calm him down. Maybe they think that makes me complicit, or they may blame me for failing to put the 'bad guys' away." He walked to the board to stand beside her. "Maybe the killer never considered the investigators as culpable, never felt any rage toward us until—"

"Until they saw you in Burke's Garden, recognized you, and reacted in a spontaneous rage. Chances are high they followed you to the sheriff's department and then home."

"And planned to kill me like—" He whirled and headed for his desk. Snatching up his phone, he placed a call. "Val, have them test the victims specifically for Rohypnol, see if they can find any traces of it." He listened then hung up. "If it was at my house and at the coal processing plant, we may have a link."

*Rohypnol? At Noah's?* Kelsie grabbed the back of the chair. She drew a shaky breath, trying to hold herself together. "Noah? Someone brought… They showed up at your house with…"

He settled the phone back to the desk and came to her, but he didn't touch her. "With a syringe full of it. Enough to kill me."

She swallowed hard, forcing the coffee to stay

in her stomach. "So they're killing with Rohypnol." This must have been one of those things he felt she didn't need to know. There was no time to wonder now why he'd kept her in the dark.

She scanned the board, trying to hold herself together, trying to stay upright. "And the way a serial killer's mind works..." The girl who'd died at the party had probably been drugged with Rohypnol. Which meant... "Noah?" She didn't want to ask the question. "Was she..."

He laced his fingers with hers and drew her to him.

She didn't fight. She felt the need to be held, to be safe...

To let Noah help her through.

His embrace was sure and steady. His heart beat against her chest.

Her eyes drifted closed. She was strong, she could stand on her own, but it felt so good to let someone else hold her up.

He turned his head and spoke against her hair. "Kels...she was."

The coffee cup slid from her fingers and clattered to the floor. She grabbed Noah around the waist and held on tight. That girl...she'd endured the horror...and she'd died.

She'd died.

They stayed in place, arms around one another, until his phone blared from his desk.

Planting a kiss on the top of her head, Noah

slipped away. His gaze never leaving hers, he answered and listened.

His eyes went wide, and he killed the call without saying a word. Shock and grief tightened his expression.

"What?" At this point, she wasn't sure she could take any more surprises.

Noah opened his mouth, closed it, then finally spoke. "Kelsie... Will's dead."

As Kelsie navigated the route to the bar where Will had been found dead near his truck, Noah scrolled through the New Year's case file on his phone and tried to focus.

It was tough. His heart kept trying to wrest control from his brain.

Kelsie had taken his coffee.

She'd let him hold her.

What was happening?

This woman, this amazing woman, whose trust in him and in everyone else in the world had been shot full of holes...had trusted *him*.

Again.

*God, what am I supposed to do with this?*

None of it computed, yet here they were.

Because she trusted him.

He'd expected the news that Corinna Phillips had been drugged and assaulted to send her running in a renewal of her own pain and fear.

Instead, she'd stepped into his open arms and let him comfort her.

Her simple act of trust had ripped open something inside of him, something he'd been burying for years. Something he'd had to force down with ever-increasing force since their midnight conversation, when the truth had finally flowed and she'd given him a glimpse into her *why*.

*Lord, I still love her.*

Against all odds, he did.

And by trusting him, she'd ripped away his last doubts, though his fears still raged. Could she love him in return? Did she want to? Was it—

"Who would kill Will? He wasn't there that night, according to you and what you've read in your report." Kelsie steered the car around a curve with one hand. Strangely, she still had a death grip on his travel mug, which she'd swiped from the floor as they were rushing out of the office.

"I don't know. But, Kels?" He'd held back info, not on purpose but because his mind had been trying to process what was happening. "He was found outside the bar. There's not a mark on him."

She swung her gaze to his. "Drugged?"

"Or he could have accidentally overdosed or had a heart attack or any number of things. As of right now, you know as much as I do." All Val had told him was Will was dead outside of a bar and to get there as quickly as possible, because there was more she didn't want to tell him over the phone.

She'd also warned him off bringing Kelsie, but what was he supposed to do? She was right there with him. He couldn't leave her alone in her vulnerable state, could he?

Why wouldn't Val want Kelsie there?

Kelsie had hinted she was suspicious of Val but, really, she had no reason to be. If Val wanted him dead, she could have killed him a hundred times over. And she wasn't linked to the case they suspected had triggered the killer, so there was also that.

Taking a deep breath, he forced his focus back to his phone. It had been a few years, but he could remember a gaggle of teenagers, shaken and crying. Others on scene who had more experience had spoken with them while he'd spent his time talking to Will, who'd just turned eighteen. He'd been horrified by the death and terrified of the police.

Corinna had been found in the master bathroom on the far end of the house from the party. The coroner determined she'd been drugged with Rohypnol and assaulted, but something had gone wrong and she'd died from an overdose. There had never been enough evidence to link anyone present to the crime, and the case had gone cold.

Until now. Someone knew something and, rather than take that information to law enforcement, they'd chosen revenge.

He switched to a different screen. "I'm going to

check witness interviews, see if any names jump off the page."

"Sounds like there could be any number of people who—"

"Wait." Adrenaline hit his system when a familiar name appeared on the list, seeming to flash brighter than the others. "Kelsie..."

"You found something." She looked at him then back to the road, her forehead wrinkled in concentration and concern.

He quickly scanned the list for any other familiar names but found none, but the one he'd found had a connection to the party and to Jaxon Collins. He'd have never imagined it if he wasn't staring straight at it.

Kelsie waited patiently as he called a colleague, Agent Brian Mowse. He didn't even wait for Brian to fully say hello. "Mowse, I'm headed to a crime scene, but I need you to work on bringing a person of interest in for a chat." He glanced at Kelsie. "Priscilla Lambert." Kelsie gasped, but he kept speaking. "Aged twenty-five. Works at the soda shop in Bramwell." He quickly sketched out other information and his reasons for wanting to speak to her.

"Got it. That gives me enough to get the ball rolling. I'll get back to you when I have something." Mowse ended the call without saying goodbye.

When he lowered his phone, Kelsie looked at

him. "Priscilla? The blonde waitress that..." She shook her head, her jaw tight, and turned her attention back to the road. The attacker had always worn oversized clothing and had operated on the element of surprise, but still... How had they missed it was a woman? "She was the one who gave us intel about Jaxon running afoul of a bunch of guys she couldn't describe on a trip she couldn't give us an exact date for."

"She set us up to chase our tails." He was angry with himself, angry with Priscilla... How had me missed that?

He'd missed it because no one would ever have suspected the seemingly terrified young woman. They'd had no reason to.

But it had all been right there if they'd known where to look. "She even had opportunity to come after me in Bramwell. The cook, Braden, said they brought their ATVs in and went out on the trails after work. She would have had time to get to one and to run me down." He texted that detail to Mowse. There wasn't time now to follow up on it himself. They were pulling up to their newest crime scene.

The Drunken Goat Roadhouse was an old white two-story farmhouse off 77 that had been gutted and turned into a restaurant and bar frequented by locals. It wasn't the kind of place known for "day drinking," but given Will's state of mind, he'd probably driven to the nearest place to escape his family and his grief.

In the process, he may have run headlong into a killer.

Crime scene tape ringed the parking lot.

Kelsie nodded toward a dark green SUV by the road. "That's Elliott. I told him we were headed here. Think you can get him in?"

"Sure." Noah held up his badge to an officer who guarded the entrance and explained who Elliott was. The officer waved them through then gave the high sign to Elliott, who climbed out of his vehicle and ducked under the crime scene tape.

He was waiting for them when they parked.

Noah hung back as Kelsie greeted her boss, studying their interaction. She seemed at ease with the tall, broad-shouldered former soldier. A close-cropped beard covered the lower half of the man's face, and his dark hair grew nearly to his collar. He carried himself with an easy confidence edged with a wariness that said, though he appeared to be relaxed, he was observing everything and could leap into action at a moment's notice.

Jury was out on whether or not he was likable.

Elliott stood close enough to Kelsie to indicate they were more than acquaintances, but he maintained a professional distance.

Maybe he was a *little* likable.

Kelsie waved Noah over. "Elliott, this is Special Agent Noah Cross with the Virginia State Police Bureau of Criminal Investigation. Noah, this is Elliott Weiss, owner of Trinity Investigations."

The men clasped hands.

Elliott didn't seem to be familiar with Noah's name, which meant Kelsie had likely never spoken of him.

Why would she? He was old news.

The thought cut deeper than he wanted.

Noah swallowed his slight jealousy as he withdrew his hand. "Thanks for the help on this. I know you got dragged into it because our cases crossed, but it's good to have fresh eyes."

Elliott nodded. "Kelsie says you might have another victim on your hands."

"We might." With a nod, Noah turned toward the parking lot, where multiple official vehicles sat. The coroner was near the back of a blue late-model Super Duty pickup truck, likely Will's vehicle. "I think we've put together who might be—"

"Cross." Val strode up, her expression cloudy.

Noah eyed her, trying to work through Kelsie's suspicions. Val had no motive and, a few times, no opportunity. Kelsie had to be wrong.

She gave him a curious look, as though she could read his mind, then seemed to brush off whatever she was thinking. In her hand, she held an evidence bag containing what appeared to be a napkin. Her gaze flicked to Kelsie and Elliott. "Didn't we talk on the phone?"

*Didn't I tell you not to bring Kelsie?* He heard the words loud and clear, but he ignored them. He hadn't had a lot of choice, though Val wouldn't see it that way. He introduced her to Elliott then tipped his head toward the pickup. "What have we got?"

If looks could kill... Val took a deep breath and seemed to resign herself to the fact that they would have company. She turned to Noah as though Kelsie and Elliott didn't exist. "Will Daugherty arrived around two this afternoon. He had a few drinks, then chatted up a young woman who arrived shortly after him. She didn't stay long, and after she left, he staggered out of the bar. Owner followed him to take his keys and found him by the vehicle, unresponsive. By the time EMS arrived, it was too late. Given the current situation, the coroner is leaning toward an overdose of some sort. We're getting a warrant for the security camera footage, but we're focused on the woman."

"Let me guess." Kelsie stepped up beside him. "She was slightly below average height. Blonde. Bartender probably described her as 'cute.'"

Val's left eyebrow arched. She was impressed. "How did you know that?"

Noah took over. "Because we may know who's behind all of this." He filled Val in on their discovery. "I'm having Mowse look into Priscilla's relationship to Corinna Phillips and having her brought in as a person of interest."

The pieces were falling into place, but one thing

still puzzled him. Val had accepted Kelsie's interjection without protest, but she'd not initially wanted her to come along.

He gave Val a hard look, shifting his gaze to Kelsie in silent question.

Val looked away, her mouth drawn into a tight line, but not in anger. It was something else.

Silently, she handed him the evidence bag she'd been holding.

The world seemed to move in slow motion as he took it. Whatever this was, it involved Kelsie, and it wasn't good.

Angling so Kelsie couldn't see over his shoulder, he looked down. A napkin was sealed inside the bag. He flipped it over, and his heart dropped into his shoes.

A message had been scrawled in ballpoint pen across the napkin. *Kelsie, this is justice for you.*

# FOURTEEN

Something was wrong...and it was about her.

As Noah let the evidence bag drop to his side, something radiated off him that Kelsie couldn't quite place.

But it was Elliott who concerned her most. His height and angle had allowed him to see over Noah's shoulder. He knew what was in that evidence bag, and it had set his face in stone.

He turned to her with a wrinkled brow full of questions and possibly some anger. "Kelsie?"

She took a step back. Did they think she had something to do with this? She'd been with Noah all morning. The fear that zipped through her had nothing to do with her past and everything to do with right now. Was she about to be framed? Why? "Noah?" He'd be honest with her. If she'd learned nothing else over the course of the past few days, it was that she could still trust Noah Cross.

He didn't move. Didn't speak. When he finally shifted his gaze, it was to stare at Will's pickup truck. His mind was working. It seemed as if he was trying to do math that didn't quite add up.

But then his eyes closed and he breathed deeply as though he was steeling himself.

As strong as she was, Kelsie couldn't take the suspense any longer. "Tell me." She stepped between him and Val and forced him to look at her. "Now."

"Kelsie." Elliott used his *I'm your boss* voice.

She didn't care. "Noah. Show me."

"Show her." Val's voice was quiet. "I don't know what it means, but..." She spoke as though she was trying to beat down some sort of emotion. Sadness? Regret?

Nothing made sense.

Noah held the evidence bag out to her, holding her gaze. "I'm right here."

What did that mean?

She grasped the bag and glanced at Elliott, who watched her as though he was wary of what she might do next.

Her heart hammered. Her palms were damp. She looked down.

*Kelsie, this is justice for you.*

Justice? How was someone murdering Will Daugherty justice for—

A lightning bolt struck. Her entire body jolted with the shock. She couldn't breathe. Couldn't think. Her hands shook. Her insides quaked.

*No.*

Shoving the bag into Noah's chest, she stepped back and bumped into Elliott's shoulder.

There were no words, just a screaming flight response.

Whirling, she dashed to her vehicle and around to the far side, away from prying eyes. She doubled over and rested her hands on her knees, gulping air, fighting nausea, wrestling the darkness encroaching on her vision.

She was going to pass out.

Kelsie the Brave, Kelsie the Strong, Kelsie who had it all together was splintering in front of everyone.

Sinking to the ground, she buried her face in her knees, wrapped her arms around her legs and tried to make herself as small as possible.

Will Daugherty had been the one to—

*God, help me.*

Having a faceless attacker, a disembodied voice had been one thing. But to put a face to...to the nightmare? The horror? The shame?

Moaning, she doubled over tighter. She didn't want to be sick.

She wanted to be numb. To be well. To be anywhere but here.

Footsteps crunched on gravel, and someone settled beside her.

Kelsie tensed. *Don't touch me. Please.* She couldn't bear for Noah to see her like this. For her boss to see her like this. For—

"I know what you're feeling." It wasn't Noah or Elliott. It was Val.

Kelsie stiffened but didn't respond. Val had no idea.

"Right now—" the other woman's tone was low and calm "—you're either wanting to run away or to crawl into the smallest space you can find so no one can reach you. The fear and the shame are drowning you. It's all there, as fresh as the moment..." Her voice dropped impossibly low. "As the moment it happened."

The declaration, the *knowing*, slammed the brakes on the panic attack threatening to rip Kelsie apart. Turning her head, she rested her cheek on her knee and stared at the woman beside her. How did she know?

One look at Val's face, and there was no denying it. "It happened to you."

"In college." Val's gaze never wavered. Her jaw was set, yet her eyes held the kind of sympathy only a fellow survivor could feel. "I was on a date with a guy I thought I knew."

An ache rose behind Kelsie's eyes. The tears she had never been able to cry welled up and burst out in an ugly cry. "I never knew who he was. Now I have..." The sobs pulsed up and out, shaking through her. "A face." The words tore at her throat. Though the memories didn't change, they muscled their way through her mind's eye, insisting on adding Will's face.

Val inhaled and exhaled loudly. "Is it okay if I put my hand on your shoulder?"

The kindness, the thoughtfulness of asking, dropped Kelsie's head even lower. She could only nod, humiliated she was crying.

Relieved she was crying.

Val rested her hand on Kelsie's shoulder, warm and comforting, and simply sat with her as the tears flowed.

A valve that had shut sixteen years earlier opened, and the waters poured forth. The tension she'd held in every nerve ending eased. Her muscles relaxed.

It felt as though she'd shed a two-hundred-pound weight that had been pushing against her skin from the inside out.

The storm was intense but short-lived. When Kelsie could breathe again, she dropped her head back against the side of her SUV and stared across the road at the woods on the other side. Cars zipped past out of sight on the highway. On the other side of the SUV, officers and investigators worked. For what felt like the first time in her life, she could distinguish individual sights and sounds and thoughts instead of just the screams of the past that tried to bust through her defenses.

As Val pulled her hand away, Kelsie studied her. "You didn't kill Will or the others, did you?"

"No." The other woman smiled gently, not offended by the question. "I can see why you'd be suspicious. I've been in close proximity to Noah almost every time someone came at him."

Kelsie nodded, then rolled her head to stare up at the sky. The SUV seemed to be the only thing holding her up. "How did you..." She waved her hand to encompass the entire world.

"Survive?" Val bent her knees to mimic Kelsie's posture. Those dress pants were going to be a wreck when she got up off the gravel. "He was arrested and, while it wasn't a strong enough punishment, he was convicted and spent a bit of time in jail. I had friends who rallied around me and got me help. Counseling. A whole lot of time with Jesus. It took me a long, long time to trust Him again. To tell Him I was angry with Him for letting it happen."

"I know that anger well." It still burned. Even tears hadn't doused it.

"I've seen Him use everything I went through though. Not that I would ever want to go through it again, ever, but... If I hadn't, who would be sitting with you right now?"

This was true. Though she'd kept her own pain locked inside, she'd sat with countless female soldiers in their aftermaths. She'd sat with Rebecca and given her a sense of normalcy after she was poisoned.

"In a perfect world, where sin didn't exist, no one would need someone to sit beside them, but the world isn't perfect, and we need someone. I needed someone. But, Kelsie, God didn't make this happen to you. Sin exists. People do horrible things. In God's hands, those horrible things can be redeemed and passed on to help others going through horrible things."

God really had used her trauma to help others, like Joseph in the Bible. Like others. Like she'd begun to wonder if He might use her.

The truth made her head pound. "I don't know what to do with this."

"I think you heal." Val picked up a piece of gravel and weighed it in her hand. "For too long, your nightmare had no face, which meant it could be any man. Deep inside, every man could be the man who hurt you."

Something settled over her mind. Was Val onto something? Could she truly begin to heal now that the monster had a face?

"Kelsie, I'll be honest. I work alongside good men like Noah and your boss, Elliott. Over the years, I've learned not every man is evil. Not every man will hurt me. It helps to know good men, considering the nature of our pasts and our job." She leaned her shoulder against Kelsie's, her voice lifting. "Elliott's not bad to look at, by the way."

Kelsie's laugh surprised her. She covered her mouth at the unladylike snort, grateful for the levity. "Don't even try. He's a confirmed bachelor."

"Like you're a confirmed bachelorette? Then

I'm not too worried. I don't see you lasting much longer in the single category." She winced. "I'm sorry. You're reliving a major trauma and I—"

"Don't. I need to be distracted." Kelsie stood, brushed off her jeans, then held her hand out to Val and helped her up. "I can unpack this later. For now, we need to figure out exactly what happened to W—" Nausea rocked her again. A face. A name. The truth.

Another death.

She grabbed the side of the SUV and waited a second for the world to right itself. It would take so much more time, so much more talking, so much more everything before she was okay. She could see that now.

Val reached for her. "You okay?"

She nodded, and the waviness passed. "It's a lot to take in."

"Whatever you need, I'm here. I know it's a long road. It winds through a lot of mountains and valleys. Sometimes it's better and sometimes..." Val offered a smile. "Just know I'm here. And I suspect Noah is, too."

The sentiment moved Kelsie, but she was out of tears. She needed to get outside of her head until she was alone and could process. Maybe she even needed to pray. She wasn't sure of anything anymore. "I need to focus on work, something I can control. Something like seeing if the bartender recognizes a photo of Priscilla Lambert." She was one hundred percent certain he would. But that begged a whole other question... How had Priscilla known that Will had—

Her mind couldn't handle it. Not right now.

"I'll pull up her social media." Val looked up from her phone as Kelsie walked to the front of her SUV and looked across the parking lot. "And you need time to go process. You don't want to, but you need to."

"Maybe..." Kelsie stared across the parking lot.

Noah was talking to Elliott and another agent near Will's truck, where a crime scene tech was taking photos. As though he could feel her gaze, Noah glanced over his shoulder, his brow furrowed in concern.

How much effort had it taken for Val to keep him from following her? There was no doubt he would have, that he was the one who'd wanted to take care of her all along, who would never purposely let her down.

Val was right. She needed to go back to the apartment and think. To figure this out. To consider—

Val inhaled sharply. "Kelsie?" Slowly, she turned her phone and held it up. "This is Priscilla Lambert?"

Kelsie nodded, grateful to be pulled from her thoughts but concerned by Val's expression.

"We'll show this to the bartender, but she has to be our suspect." Val looked at the photo again.

"She's the one who handed over the pizza and drinks. She's the one who drugged Noah."

He should have gone with Kelsie.

Noah pulled up to the field office and shut off the engine to Kelsie's borrowed SUV, but he didn't get out of the vehicle. He stared at the lighted window of Val's office, trying to put a thousand scattered thoughts into neat little boxes.

Will Daugherty had cost Kelsie everything.

Will Daugherty had cost Noah everything.

Will Daugherty was dead. The thoughts refused to be contained, and they tangled with the information Mowse had passed along earlier, further twisting his logic.

Priscilla Lambert was Corinna Phillips's stepsister. She'd been at the party when Corinna died. She'd been the one to find her dead in that bathroom.

He'd investigated a lot of heinous crimes, but this one felt so much more vile and evil, not merely because of the murders but because of the catalyst for them. Priscilla was avenging the helpless, the broken...

*Oh, God, it's so much wrong and so much pain.*

He wanted it to make sense, but he couldn't fathom the mind of a man who took what he wanted, nor could he process killing in an effort to make things right.

He needed Kelsie. She helped him think, helped him see more clearly.

Maybe she even helped him heal.

He dragged his hands down his face. At Val's insistence, Kelsie had left the crime scene with Elliott, handing the keys to her SUV to Noah as she'd passed and promising to be in touch later.

She needed time away, to work through the truths she'd learned and the wounds those truths had ripped open.

Why did it feel like he had lost her? Was she coming apart? Pulling it together? Was she still in Virginia or had she fled to North Carolina in the face of her renewed trauma?

Was she healing? Or was she dying?

Was he wrong to be here? Should he be beside her?

There were too many questions and no good answers.

He glanced at his phone. There was a string of information from the crime scene techs, the coroner and Val, but nothing personal, nothing from Kelsie. He'd refrained from texting her because he wanted to give her space, but would that make her think he didn't care? Or would she appreciate the thoughtfulness?

*Ugh.* He shoved his phone into his interior jacket pocket. More questions.

For now, he needed to get inside and start working through evidence with Val. It was going to be another long night. He wasn't sure how many more of those he could handle.

His phone pinged as he opened the SUV's door. *Kelsie?*

With one foot on the pavement, he pulled the phone out and tapped the screen.

An update on the search for Priscilla Lambert. The bartender had confirmed she'd been the woman with Will at the bar, but she'd vanished. She'd not gone home or to work.

Sean had confirmed she'd left the soda shop shortly after they had the day before, claiming she felt sick. That gave her ample time to be on the ATV that had nearly run him down and to make her way to the coal processing plant. They'd probably surprised her during an attempt at cleaning up.

The pizza place had confirmed their driver had handed off their delivery to someone matching Priscilla's description outside the field office. It seemed she'd then drugged their drinks and posed as the delivery driver.

So where was she now? And why was she after him?

He surveyed the area. If he was Priscilla's target, she could be anywhere. She'd proven she could take down grown men, and he should be more careful than to sit here with no backup and with his attention focused on his phone.

Scanning the small lot, he exited the vehicle,

then headed for the building, sliding past Val's car, which was parked in the next spot.

How had such a small young woman been able to get a man like Jaxon Collins up those stairs?

He rolled his eyes toward the sky as he unlocked the door. *The drugs.* If she'd given Jaxon Collins enough to make him compliant and then promised him—

Yeah, Jaxon had likely followed her right up those steps, shaky and weak, thinking he was going to be rewarded at the top.

Instead, he'd been imprisoned and murdered.

Val theorized Priscilla had drugged each of her victims, putting them through the same torture she believed her stepsister had endured as the drugs robbed them of their sanity. Each victim had ultimately faced death and lost. Priscilla had targeted anyone who she'd deemed guilty.

But there had been several first responders and investigators. Why him?

Noah shoved open the door then locked it behind him. The warm air inside the building blasted him. Val was the queen of turning up the heat. He liked the temp to be more like an icebox.

"Val?" He shucked off his coat, hung it on the coatrack by the door, then headed up the dark hallway toward her office, where the only light in the building blazed.

She didn't respond.

He reached for the hall light switch but hesitated. Something felt off. The building wasn't that big. She should be able to hear him.

It was possible she'd dropped off her car and run to get food with someone else, but she'd have told him her plans, since they'd agreed to meet. Even if she was in the bathroom, she'd acknowledge his presence.

The hairs on his arms rose. He reached for his sidearm and wrapped his fingers around the grip as he flicked the tab on the holster. He drew the weapon and held it low.

Slowly, he crept toward Val's office, his ears attuned to every sound in the small building.

At the door, he pressed his back to the wall and waited a beat before entering, sweeping the room with gun and gaze.

No one was inside.

His scanned the room, then the floor.

At the corner of the desk, Val's legs were visible.

*No.*

He took one step toward her.

The lights went out.

Before he could whirl, a sharp jab punched into his neck. He spun, but it was too late. The drug was already taking effect.

The world slid sideways. His knees went weak. His gun clattered to the ground. The darkness deepened...

# FIFTEEN

"I'm surprised you never said anything." Elliott sat on her couch, seeming to take up all the space in the tiny apartment. He was working his way through the truth about the burden she'd silently carried for so long. "Kelsie, your team would have helped you, would have had your back."

"I know, but some things don't come easily, especially for people like us." People who were strong, who handled everything thrown at them, who defended and protected those who needed help. The army had taught them that. Working for Trinity had reinforced it. Pulling out a chair in the dining area, Kelsie sank into it. "I dealt with the…" She exhaled loudly and sat back, sliding her hands to her thighs and holding on tight. She'd probably never be able to say the words, not about her own assault. "I thought I'd handled it, but coming back here and facing it…" She shrugged. "It's been harder than I expected."

"I can imagine, especially if you haven't been here since then. That's a long time to build up the trauma in your head and let it grow to mythological proportions."

That was something she'd never considered. Withholding her past from her team had kept her from using it to fully help others, but it had also allowed the fear to feed in the darkness until it grew into a monster that devoured her life. "I never thought of it that way."

"It let your trust issues fester, too." He tipped his head toward her. "Don't think I haven't seen it."

She looked away, down at the floor. While she had often encouraged her teammates to open up to her, she'd rarely offered much about herself. Only Rebecca and their former teammate Gavin Mercer knew she'd once been a ballet dancer, but that had only slipped out after a long night of digging through insanely boring financial records when they were looking into a fraud case. If she'd been less-exhausted or less-bored she'd have never spilled that information. She could trust Rebecca not to say anything, and Gavin had moved on to a job with the FBI, so she'd never worried about anyone else finding out. Until now.

"You know…" Elliott leaned forward and rested his elbows on his knees. "Bad, awful things happen in life. They can take us down, and that's normal. We're not machines. I've seen things…" He smiled softly, sadly. "Ironically, I've seen things I haven't talked about with you guys. The only way to break their hold on us is to use them to help others."

That was exactly what Val had repeated when she'd called to check on her half an hour earlier. "I'm hearing that a lot." Kelsie dug her teeth into her lip, then looked her boss in the eye. Maybe more than a boss… Maybe a friend. "You sure you don't pray? Haven't gotten to know Jesus a little?" It felt good to mention His name without recoiling, though they still had some work to do. "You sure do talk like him. There's a whole verse in the Bible about him using things for good—"

"No. That's not up for discussion. You can all do your thing, I'm gonna do mine." He stood and looked across the small room at her. "This explains that tricked out emergency kit you keep in the back of your car, yellow safety vest and all."

She smiled. He'd teased her about that more than once. It made her feel safe when she was on back roads alone. It was proof she could take care of herself.

Elliott sobered. "We can keep talking, but I think, right now, Noah needs you. I'm pretty sure he actually might want you to stick around for a while, but that's beside the point. You and I are here to help him out. Call him. Talk about the case, talk about what happened, but call him. He was pretty wrecked when we left, I think."

Noah? Wrecked? By her?

*Right.*

Then again...there had been those moments when the air between them had charged, when the past had crept in and she'd thought maybe, if only for the shortest moment, there might still be something to hold them to one another.

"You don't trust easily, and I understand why. Someone you knew violated your safety and wreaked havoc in your life. Kelsie..." His expression clouded, and he looked away, his gaze hard. "You're one of my people, and if Daugherty was alive, I'd have words for—" He swung his hand in front of his face as though he could wipe the air clean. "I have no idea how you survived."

"I have no idea either." Now that she'd come apart, she wondered how she'd managed to hold it together for so long.

"Not Jesus?"

Kelsie sunk her teeth into her upper lip and stared at the ceiling. Had Jesus been there?

There had been a counselor who'd guided her when she could no longer dance without having a panic attack. Her fellow female soldiers who'd closed ranks around one another, shared their stories, and had one another's backs in a male-dominated profession where women weren't always respected.

There had been Val's words today.

She'd been angry with God. Furious He had allowed such horrible things to happen to her, that He'd left her alone in that dark room. And yet He'd been there all along, providing what she needed, helping her heal, giving her strength. "Honestly, I'm pretty sure He was there, too."

"Hm." Elliott stood. "Call Noah. We'll head over to the field office to help them like we're being paid to do. I think the personal part of this conversation is done for now."

Maybe that was okay.

Besides, she had a lot of personal things to say to Noah.

As her fingers landed on her phone in her hip pocket, the device vibrated with an incoming call. She glanced at the screen then held it up for Elliott to see. "It's Val." She pulled the phone to her ear. "Hello?"

The line rustled, and indistinct voices filtered through, as though they were in another room. It sounded like a woman talking.

Must be a butt dial.

She moved to end the call, but the volume suddenly increased, as though the speaker button had been pushed.

"I wanted them to know." The woman's voice was strong and clear, forceful yet somehow ragged at the edges. "I wanted all of you to know what it felt like."

That wasn't Val's voice. It was somewhat familiar, but she couldn't place it.

Elliott started to speak, but Kelsie held up one finger and hit the *mute* button then the *speaker* button before giving him a nod. He stared at the phone. "Who is that?"

She shrugged. Whoever it was, this call was deliberate. Val wanted them to hear it. But where was she, and why wasn't she speaking?

The voice came again. It wavered slightly, as though the person speaking was in motion. A rustle indicated they might be moving around the room, perhaps pacing. "Drew Daugherty killed Corinna. He hurt her and he killed her. And nobody did anything about it."

Kelsie's sharp inhale stabbed her chest. "That's Priscilla Lambert. She's the one we think is behind all of this."

Elliott headed for the door. "Where's Val?"

Kelsie was right behind him. "When she called earlier, she said she was heading to the field office."

"Then we're going to the—"

"Now?" Priscilla spoke again, and they both stopped, Elliott's hand on the door. "Now you get to suffer like she did. You get to die like she did. Scared. In the dark. Alone."

Kelsie froze. "Elliott." Fear boomeranged in her system. "She's not talking to Val. She's not close enough to the phone. There's somebody else in the room." Her heartbeat thumped wildly, threatening to drop her to the floor. Please not now, not ever, but especially not when she was figuring everything out, when she was... "She's talking to Noah. Elliott, she's going to kill Noah."

\* \* \*

*Now you get to suffer like she did. You get to die like she did.*

The words pounded Noah's ears and bounced in his head. Had he heard them or dreamed them? Everything was dark and foggy. His arms and legs wouldn't move. They were too heavy. He couldn't lift his head.

His ears roared and buzzed. It was like his entire body had gone offline then hit a power surge.

Panic rolled through him. He couldn't breathe. Couldn't move. Couldn't do anything to help himself.

His veins felt like fire was shooting through them, hot and molten. He was burning alive. Dying.

Gasping and choking, he managed to open his eyes slightly. He was staring at his knees, his feet. He was slumped forward, being held up by pressure on his wrists, but he couldn't pull himself upright.

He wobbled from side to side, tried to lift his arms. Couldn't. Tried to move his legs. Couldn't.

He blinked and his head swiveled as though it was on a tilt-a-whirl. It felt like his brain was sloshing inside of his skull, thumping painfully against the sides.

Was he awake? Dreaming? Was he at home, on his couch, still recovering?

No, something else had happened. Something more. Some memory he couldn't—

A force shoved his forehead, the pressure slamming him back into the chair. The pressure didn't let up.

He closed his eyes against the sudden movement. "Gonna be sick."

"Good. Then you'll know how it feels." The voice was female, cutting, angry. "You didn't help Corinna, and I'm not helping you. I mean, I'll Narcan you this once, so you can enjoy the pain, but after that?"

He tried to shake off the pressure that kept him from slumping forward, but it pushed against his forehead harder. *Corinna? Who—*

*Corinna.* The name slammed into his conscious, suddenly crystal clear. Shock squelched the nausea. He fought and struggled and finally convinced his eyes to open.

Priscilla Lambert stood in front of him, her arm extended and her hand shoving his forehead back. Her expression was angry, her eyes filled with hatred. "You recognize her name?" She leaned closer, her eyes glistening in the ambient light that fell in the dark room. "You recognize her name but you did nothing to stop the man who killed her."

She jerked her hand away.

His body rebounded, lurching forward in the chair. The nausea was quick to return, and he wrestled it with everything he had. He might not be in full control, but he wouldn't fully lose control either.

What was happening?

Priscilla paced the room. He could hear her moving behind him, but he couldn't see her, couldn't seem to track her position past the ringing in his ears. What had happened? How had he gotten here? Why was everything dark—

*Wait*. He'd come in. The office lights were on. He'd seen— "Val." Her name barely made it past his dry throat and mouth.

"Your partner?" The voice came from over his left shoulder, close, as though she'd leaned down and was talking near his ear. "She'll be fine. I didn't want to dose her. Didn't want her to suffer." Priscilla's voice took on a tinge of regret. "I had no choice. She's a lot like Kelsie, trained to fight. She'll come around." Her voice hardened and she grabbed the back of his head, shoving him forward, causing the world to rock. "But you won't."

Noah tried to steady himself. She was going to kill him.

And there was no help coming. No one knew they were in this predicament. He had to get himself out of this, had to get her talking to buy himself some time. "Why?"

"Why?" Her voice shrilled higher, cracking with anger. She walked in front of him, her boots appearing in his vision.

Noah took a deep breath and forced his head back so he could look his would-be killer in the eye. If he could keep her gaze locked, he could perhaps keep her from watching the rest of his movements too closely. Maybe he could work his hands free. "How did you kill those people? Why?"

"Why?" Her emotional state was clearly off the charts. She stepped away, and Noah tugged at his wrists. Maybe he could—

No. She'd used his and Val's handcuffs to restrain him to the chair. Unless he could break the wooden arm, which would call attention to himself before he could succeed, he was stuck. *Come on, Val. Wake up. Get us out of this.*

Or someone else needed to come in. But would she kill anyone who happened to stumble into the building? She likely had both of their weapons, and in the state she was in—

She whirled toward him, staying several feet away. "Corinna died because of them. That clerk, he sold alcohol to a bunch of us. He fueled that party. He made things go sideways. And that drug-dealing lowlife? He was there. He sold the drugs to Drew. And Drew..." Her voice shuddered. Tough to tell if it was grief or rage. "He used them on Corinna. He did that to her. He hurt her. She died. She died because of him. She was scared and alone and hurt and she died."

Noah said nothing, just watched as her eyes

glazed over while she stared into the past at things he couldn't see. "I wanted them to feel what she felt, so I shot them up, and I left them alone in the dark to die. I left them afraid."

"In the tower?" How had she gotten them all up and down those steps?

"No." Her gaze snapped back to his. "Only Drew and Jackson in the tower. Because they needed to feel it the worst. I promised them things, got them there, then shot them up and brought them back, over and over, until they couldn't take it anymore and they gave up." Her mouth twitched in what might have been the start of a smile before her expression shifted to anger. "They needed to feel that terror, that fear, of being alone, in the dark and terrified. Of being out of control. Of being at someone else's mercy when they couldn't fend for themselves. They paid for what they did to Corinna. It was justice."

"And Will?" He didn't want to hear this, but he needed time to think. He had to get out of here or she'd light his veins up with enough fentanyl or Rohypnol or whatever she'd gotten her hands on to end him.

"Will wasn't planned, not exactly." She walked to Val's desk. Reaching into a tote bag, she pulled out a syringe and a bottle and set it on the desk.

Her back was to him, and Noah tried to free his feet. If he could get his toes on the floor, he might be able to launch himself at her and end this.

"When I met Kelsie at the soda shop, I recognized her from seeing her dance when I was a kid. She was a star around here. I remembered... I remembered Will getting drunk at a party a few years ago and bragging about the ballerina, the 'ice queen' he went to school with, about the one time she was alone and he took what he'd always wanted. It could have only been Kelsie. She deserved justice like Corinna." She turned, syringe in hand. "You left Kelsie alone, Noah. And when you could have arrested Drew for what he did, you stood there talking to him like he was the victim. You covered up what he did. You took care of him instead of taking care of her."

"That's not what happened." He stopped trying to free himself. "We didn't know. I was there, trying to comfort a scared kid who—"

"A scared kid?" She crossed the room in two strides and grabbed his chin, shoving his head back so hard the chair rocked and his head spun. Pain shot down his spine. "Corinna was the scared kid. He was the evil monster who hurt her. Who killed her. And we're done talking." She jabbed the needle into his neck.

The pain was unfathomable.

"Goodbye, Noah."

# SIXTEEN

This was not happening.

Kelsie jammed the accelerator of Elliott's SUV to the floor. Whatever Priscilla had said after telling Noah they were done talking had been muffled, but the deathly silence that followed was the most terrifying sound she'd ever heard. "Call 911 and update them, tell them we need EMS."

"They're already on the way." Elliott was texting someone, but she had no idea who and she didn't really care. She had to get to Noah before it was too late, and it was taking centuries to travel the thirty minutes from the apartment to his field office.

*Please let us be right.* It was where Val had said she was headed and was the only place where both Val and Noah would be at the same time.

Elliott had called law enforcement as they hit the road and told them their suspicions, and a team was rolling to meet them.

Hopefully, the officers would arrive first. Hopefully they could rescue Noah and Val.

She gripped the steering wheel tighter. *Just a few more miles.* "Why isn't Val doing something? Why is she quiet?"

"Calm down, Kelsie. We're going to handle this." Elliott's voice was sympathetic, but his words had force.

He was right. The last thing she needed was to give in to emotions. She needed to be in her tactical mind if she was going to be of any help...if she was going to be a part of saving Noah.

Elliott rested his phone face down on his thigh. "Priscilla said she'd drugged Val. It's likely she's alert enough to call the last number she dialed but not alert enough to neutralize the threat."

*Perhaps.* Val was a smart woman and a good agent. Making a run at Priscilla if she was woozy or weak would only wind up bringing disaster more quickly.

Kelsie took an exit at highway speeds. They were nearly there. *Just another mile.*

But would it be too late?

Elliott grabbed the handle above the door. "I knew I should have driven. It's my truck." He muttered the words and stared straight out the window. "You're off the chain, McIlheney."

It was tough to tell if he was serious, but he wasn't wrong. She was nearly out of her mind with worry. While she wanted to be her strong and capable self, her mind was racing and her heart was pounding. The adrenaline rush hadn't let up, and it threatened to send her into cardiac arrest or a dead faint.

This was too much. This was why they told law enforcement not to get involved in cases close to their hearts, because it was impossible to focus, to think straight. This feeling...she hated it.

Yet it spoke so much.

It told her the truth.

She loved Noah. If he could steal her ability to retreat into her tactical mind, to hide from her feelings, then there was no longer any denying it.

She loved him. She'd always loved him. Deep down, she'd never stopped. So much of her anxiety and grief and pain were from burying truth, from not trusting him, from cutting him out of her life instead of letting him back in. She'd blamed him for things beyond his control.

Like this moment was beyond hers.

She couldn't rescue him any more than he could have rescued her. If he could have, he would have. He'd have sacrificed himself to protect her.

*God, forgive me.* The prayer was unbidden but one of the most sincere she'd ever prayed. It wrung out of her heart in the tears she couldn't cry.

She'd distanced herself from everyone she cared about, even the Jesus she'd fallen in love with as a teenager, but she'd needed them. She'd loved them all along.

*And God, rescue Noah.*

And if He didn't? Could she still trust Him?

She had no choice. Thanks to Val, she could look back and see the ways He'd carried her even when she'd turned her back and refused to talk to Him. He'd carry her again, even if the worst happened. Even if they were too late.

*Please don't let us be too late.*

She rounded the last turn and lifted her foot from the accelerator.

An SUV sat across their lane, blocking traffic from passing. The state police logo was emblazoned on the door.

She fought to keep her breathing even. On the one hand, law enforcement was on the scene.

On the other...

She slowed the SUV and rolled down the window. The officer walked over. "I'm going to need you to turn around."

She couldn't. She wouldn't. "I'm Kelsie McIlheney. This is Elliott Weiss. We're consulting on this case for the state. We're the ones who called in the—"

"Can I see some ID?" His expression shifted when she flashed her license at him. Elliott showed his as well.

The officer nodded. "You can pull up and join the other officers ahead, but you have to stay in your vehicle. Both your SUV and Special Agent Yewell's vehicle are on-site. A vehicle belonging to the suspect is parked up the road in the trees. A team is preparing to enter the building."

One of the steel bands around her chest relaxed slightly. Her SUV was here. At least they'd guessed correctly about Noah and Val's location.

But Priscilla was desperate if she was making her move in a state building. There was no telling what she'd do. While Kelsie desperately hoped she'd heard wrong on that phone call, the evidence said to expect the worst.

Shaking slightly, she rolled to the point where several vehicles waited out of sight of the building. A tactical team stood geared up and ready to move in.

When she parked and turned off the engine, an officer in tactical gear and a cap approached. "You our observers?"

*Observers* sounded so wrong, but she nodded and flashed her ID again.

The officer passed over a handheld radio. "You can listen in, but you can't join. Remain in your vehicle, no matter what. Understood?"

She nodded slowly, taking the radio with trembling fingers. She ached to be a part of the team moving in. She was trained to do so, and every muscle cried out for action.

It would be unwise.

The officer gave her a curt nod as he stepped back. "At the all clear, you can enter." He walked away to join his team.

Kelsie gripped the radio and looked at Elliott.

He said nothing, just reached over and laid a

hand on her shoulder, his awkward way of offering support. Or was he holding her back? Words came easy for him, but actions were a little more difficult.

She'd smile if everything didn't feel like it was falling apart.

He squeezed her shoulder and withdrew his hand. "Kelsie."

When she looked at him, he tipped his head toward the windshield.

The team was moving out.

The radio crackled to life, but she barely registered the words. Tactical plans, doors to cover, windows to cover.

After several exchanges, the radio fell silent. They were likely nearing the building and hoping to approach without being seen or heard.

The silence was decades long. Decades in which she couldn't breathe. She wanted to jump out of the car, to rush in and save Noah.

But she couldn't. It wasn't her place. It wasn't her job.

And it was killing her.

She had zero control. Zero ability to affect the outcome. Zero strength to expend in this situation.

She had to trust the team going in. To trust God.

She pulled in a deep breath, held it and released it slowly.

That didn't help, so she prayed. There weren't words, but it was the longest most heartfelt prayer she'd ever uttered. God would understand the cries of her heart, the anguish she was afraid of feeling, the love that pierced her chest.

What if—

The radio crackled to life. "State police! Show me your hands! Show me your hands!"

She reflexively reached for the door, but Elliott's grip on her shoulder stopped her. "They've got this."

A cacophony of voices blended into gibberish, obscured behind her pulse pounding in her ears.

"We need medical! Now!"

She looked at Elliott. *All clear. Say all clear.*

The ambulance staged ahead of them roared to life and disappeared in the direction of the building.

Silence.

So much silence.

"All clear."

Kelsie didn't bother to start the SUV. She tossed the radio to Elliott and ran around the corner into the small parking lot with Elliott close behind.

The ambulance was near the building, its rear doors open. Medics were nowhere to be seen.

She froze. An ambulance meant he was alive, right? She looked at Elliott with the question in her eyes, but he was staring across the parking lot.

Two officers were putting Priscilla Lambert into a vehicle.

The other woman looked up and spotted Kelsie.

"I got justice for you! I got justice for Corinna!" The two officers wrestled her into the vehicle and shut the door.

Kelsie looked away, her stomach twisting. The young woman truly thought she'd done something heroic and honorable. "That's not justice." Five people were dead, all in the name of revenge. "If she'd told the truth from the start, if she'd asked for help…" She looked at Elliott, who was still watching the vehicle where Priscilla was being held. "Things would have been different."

Shouts from the building jerked her attention. Two medics rushed out with a stretcher. One was pumping a resuscitation bag to the prone person on the stretcher.

Noah.

He wasn't breathing. They were breathing for him. They were—

She tried to rush forward, but Elliott pulled her back. "Let's go. We'll follow them."

*No.* She couldn't speak, struggled to break free, but Elliott's grip tightened as the ambulance roared away.

It was a cliché he was thinking too often, but he wanted the license plate of the truck that hit him.

Noah groaned as he was dragged out of deep sleep by pain that pulsed through every nerve and muscle with every heartbeat. His head pounded.

His body ached. Even his blood burned in his veins.

He struggled for a deep breath, but the pain was too much.

His memory was shot. Where was he, and how had he gotten here? The last thing he remembered was...

Was...

Darkness? The lights going out? Something about Val?

There was nothing but vague images.

Panic rocked through him like an explosion. He was in danger. Val was in danger. Or was Kelsie in danger?

With a gasp, he forced his eyes open. "Kelsie." He tried to cry out for her, but his lungs wouldn't give him the air to do more than whisper.

He was in a semidark room, lying in a bed. Monitors glowed softly beside him. Someone moved around the bed to stand beside him. His eyes were so bleary he could barely make her out.

But it wasn't Kelsie. This woman's hair was short and blond. Her pink scrubs seemed to match her bright smile. "Well, Special Agent Cross. Welcome back to the real world. You're about to make some people in the waiting room very happy." She leaned slightly closer, bringing the scent of rubbing alcohol and soap with her. "Do you know where you are?"

He tried to shake his head, but the room tilted.

*Okay, bad idea.* "Hospital?" His voice croaked past a dry throat and cottony mouth.

"Close enough. Let's try something easier. Name?"

"Noah Thomas Cross."

She nodded. "Date?"

Was she serious? He wanted someone to give *him* answers, not be spouting out random facts to questions he didn't know the answers to.

"Come on, Special Agent Cross. You know the date." She coaxed him gently, though her forehead creased slightly.

"Everything hurts."

"I'm sure it does. We'll try to get you something for the pain soon. But the date?"

"Water?"

After she offered him a few sips through a straw, he closed his eyes, feeling somewhat more human as the cool liquid slipped down his throat. Christmas had passed. There was something about New Years's flitting around, but he couldn't catch it. "January…something." She dared not ask him what day of the week it was. He had no clue.

He only had one question of import. "Where's Kelsie? Is she safe?"

"Ironic you're asking that." The nurse smiled down at him. "She's fine. You're the one we've been worried about. You took a heavy hit of some nasty drugs. You're blessed EMS was on-site. You're young and strong and should recover fine, but you've got a couple of broken ribs. You'll recover fine, but it'll be a rocky few days."

"I was... Was I in a fight?" Why couldn't he remember?

She was halfway to the door. "Nope. CPR." She disappeared into the hallway.

*Wait. What?* She dropped a bomb like that and then left? CPR? Had he... Had he died?

"Hey."

The soft voice from the door snagged his attention.

Yep, he'd died, because Kelsie was here and, yet another cliché, she had to be an angel.

She eased into the room and stood near his head. "How are you feeling?"

"Like I fought a grizzly bear and lost." He'd been in the hospital before, when he had his appendix removed. There was a remote somewhere that would raise his head. He didn't like talking to Kelsie while he was flat on his back. It made him feel weak.

"Or like you got tackled playing football?" Her voice held a smile.

The words snagged on a memory. Walking in Bramwell, the ATV, her acting like her old self for the first time in...in forever. He chuckled, but pain shot through him and put a quick end to that. "Don't. And find a way to sit me up."

Memories were coming back slowly, but the

last one he could really grasp was leaving her at a crime scene.

At the scene of Will Daugherty's homicide.

Beyond that, there was nothing. As his head raised, his vision whirled. Vague impressions scattered across his thoughts, but none of them settled. There was danger. Fear. A menacing presence.

Something about Val.

"Is Val okay?"

"She's fine." Kelsie laid the remote beside him and sat down in a chair. "She was treated and released. Priscilla didn't dose her nearly as much as you." She winced. "You probably don't remember anything."

"No." He didn't dare shake his head. Bad enough he was flat on his back and helpless. He didn't need to add sick on top of it.

"Don't try right now." She slipped her hand into his, and her touch quieted his flipping emotions. "I'll tell you everything later. Right now…" Her fingers were warm in his, right and real and perfect. "Rest."

His eyes slipped closed. It was pretty much all he could do.

And everything else could wait. Because she was here, she was real, and nothing else mattered.

# SEVENTEEN

It was tough to believe this whole thing was finally over. Priscilla was in custody, and although she was giving up the names of several dealers who'd sold her Rohypnol, flipping on them would never be enough for the law to exonerate her for five murders. She'd never threaten anyone again.

Noah took a sip of coffee from his travel mug and surveyed his small domain, reveling in a sense of peace he'd never bothered to appreciate before. The threatened snow had finally fallen, blanketing the world in white that reflected the light like diamonds.

Sitting in his backyard now, it was hard to forget the last time he'd taken time to be still. Since he was a kid, his family had lived looking over their shoulders, and he'd continued to do that throughout his life. Though the threat was essentially nonexistent, old habits died hard.

That might be a good thing, since death had crept into the woods around his home and crossed the threshold into his sanctuary.

Had Kelsie felt this sort of fear? As though she couldn't relax because a safe place, safe people, had let her down?

Even though the air was freezing, he'd come out onto his patio with his Bible for some quiet reflection and a whole lot of thanksgiving for protection over the past few days, even though he couldn't remember much of what had happened.

But his mind kept wandering to Kelsie. Her return and the revelations about the past had thrown him for a loop even Rohypnol couldn't match. The dual druggings and the emotional strain of the past few days had done a number on the way his mind worked, but things were gradually clearing up.

Prayer was helping.

He looked to the sky and eyed heavy clouds that promised more snow. Their first snowfall had been so late this year, and he hadn't realized how much his soul yearned for it, for normalcy and predictability and the way a fresh white blanket transformed the world and covered over the rough spots. Everything was soft and clean, pure and new. The reflected light dispelled the shadows and made the world seem twice as bright.

He took a deep breath of icy cold air, wincing against pain that reminded him he'd nearly died at the hands of revenge. Had Priscilla done things the right way and gone to the police with the truths she'd used to stoke the fires of pain and anger, this would have gone differently, she wouldn't be in jail, her life in shambles while other families grieved the destruction she'd caused. Justice would have been served properly, not as she'd determined it should be.

He glanced at his Bible. This was why forgiveness was important, and he knew he needed to forgive himself. Kelsie's pain at Will's hands had left Noah with a guilt he couldn't quite release. He needed to sit with it and work through it before he could do the hard work of handing it over to God.

But not today. Soon though, because he had bigger plans than stewing in a past he couldn't change. He wanted to—

"You here?"

Plans that involved the woman who was rounding the corner of his house.

He moved to stand, but Kelsie waved him down. "I know it hurts. There's no need to be a gentleman today."

He eased back, then slid the chair on the other side of the table out with his foot in silent invitation. "Did you guys get the case wrapped up?" She'd spent the past five days with Elliott, finishing up their look into the Daniels case. She'd spent the past five evenings here with him. They'd stayed up until all hours, talking, catching up, getting to know one another again. And with every word, he knew...he was still deeply, madly in love with this woman. He'd never stopped.

"We're done." She settled into the chair. The

dark blue coat she wore brought out the pink of her cheeks and the blue in her eyes. Her brown hair was up in its customary ponytail, though a few pieces straggled around her face.

She made his breath catch more than a few broken ribs ever could. Every time he saw her, she was more beautiful than the last time.

But if she was done with her work… "So if you're finished…?" Then she was leaving. Going back to North Carolina and her regular life. "Are you going home?"

How was this going to work? They'd talked about a lot of things, but they hadn't discussed the future. Did something come next for them, or was this the end? Was this about closure, or did God have other things in mind, things Noah wanted more than he could express?

*Lord, don't let this be the end.* He needed some sign she was feeling the same as he was.

She stared at him for a long time, her blue eyes intense, as though she was trying to see his brain waves. Her expression was unreadable, but he could see the wheels turning in her mind. She was thinking, planning. He'd seen that look a thousand times.

Finally, she shifted in her seat and relaxed as though she'd come to a decision. "*Home* is a funny word."

"How so?" This wasn't the conversational turn he'd expected, but he'd follow her anywhere, so he took the path with her.

"I grew up here. This place runs through my veins. It built me." She scanned the yard, the clouds, something beyond the house... "It also tore me down. It didn't feel like home anymore. I never wanted to be here again, so I ran." She wrinkled her nose. "No, that's wrong. This place didn't tear me down. Will Daugherty did." It was obvious that sentence was a hard-won verbalization of her pain, one that might lead her to healing. "It's going to take time to work through that."

Noah said nothing. This was her moment.

"I thought I'd come here and triumph over the things chasing me. In a way, I guess I did, even if it wasn't the way I expected." She sniffed, then caught his gaze. "I *didn't* expect to run headlong into you. I didn't expect to forgive you or trust you or..." She smiled, and a sheen cast over her eyes. "Or to realize home is you. To figure out that, Noah, I still love you."

Her words hung in the air, soft and beautiful and exactly what he'd hoped to hear. The restlessness in him quieted. This was where he wanted to be.

"I haven't been myself lately." Kelsie slid to the edge of her chair. "I normally kick down doors and take names later. I say whatever is on my mind when it hits my brain, and it gets me into trouble. I'm about to kick down a door and say what's on my mind, but I don't think this is trouble. I think this is right." She eased off the chair and knelt in front of him, resting her hands on his knees. "I think we should get married." Her gaze never wavered.

Neither did his.

He brushed the hair from her forehead, placed a kiss against her soft skin and waited, hovering in the moment, wanting to bask in it so he never forgot it. Slowly, he slid his cheek down to rest against hers, basking in her warmth.

He brushed her lips and stilled, aware of her past pain, waiting for her to take the lead.

Kelsie's heart thudded against her chest as she breathed the same air as Noah Cross for the first time in forever.

It felt exhilaratingly new yet achingly familiar.

She hovered in the moment, letting it settle, never wanting it to end, this newfound freedom, this newfound forgiveness, this newfound desire to belong to him again.

Her heart stirred, feeling things she'd assumed were dead.

Things for Noah. Things that were right. Good gifts she'd never thought she'd deserve.

His cheek was warm against hers. She placed her hand gently against his chest, careful of his injuries, letting his heart beat against her palm. He was breathing. He was safe. He was alive.

And so was she.

She was inches away from their second first

kiss, from the first kiss she'd shared in love in sixteen years.

She tilted her head slightly and let her lips brush his, letting the thrill of it shoot straight through her before she came back and kissed him for real.

He met her halfway, joining her in the moment, in both of their healing. His hand rested on the side of her neck and he drew her closer, allowing them to sink into each other.

His heart pounded harder against her palm, and she knew he could feel her pulse against his fingers. No matter what happened next, they belonged to each other. No one would ever take that away from them again.

When they pulled apart, Noah rested his forehead against hers. "Wow."

She chuckled, joy stinging her eyes with tears. It was the same thing he'd said the first time they'd kissed in the front seat of his pickup, in the glow of a glorious sunset. That had been a kiss based on mutual friendship and trust and new love.

Like now.

Noah pulled in a shaky breath, probably still in pain from the cracked ribs, maybe feeling the same heart-stuttering and breath-stealing power that she'd felt in that kiss. "You know..." He slid his fingers to the back of her neck, ever so gently holding her close. "You stole my line."

"I did?" It was a wonder she could speak with him right here, so close.

"I should be the one kneeling in front of you."

"Really? I'd like to see you and your ribs try that." It didn't matter who knelt in front of who. It only mattered that they came to the same conclusion...

That they needed to spend the rest of their lives together.

He drew back, and his hand slipped from her neck, leaving her cold in his absence.

She started to move, but he gently grasped her shoulder. He didn't restrain her. He merely touched her, communicating that he wanted her to stay where she was.

His gentleness, his silent acknowledgment of her past pain, nearly undid her. After all she'd been through, after all *he'd* been through, he was seeing her, protecting her...even from himself.

He reached for the picnic table and picked up something, then handed it to her.

The small navy blue box was old and tattered. The edges were frayed and ragged, as though it had been handled many times.

It was the perfect size for... But there was no way. It couldn't be. "What is this?"

"Open it."

She lifted the flimsy lid. Inside rested a small diamond in a plain gold band.

It was absolutely understated, simple and perfect. "When did you get this?"

He took the box from her. "Doesn't matter. All

that matters is you're here now, and you basically asked me to marry you, so..." He held up the ring.

Her heart threatened to break, but she shoved the pain aside. He'd bought that ring sixteen years ago, and she'd robbed him of his chance to present it to her when she ran from him instead of trusting him.

But that didn't matter. What mattered was now. They'd had to endure the pain of separation, of healing, in order to be the people they were now and the team they would be.

Giving the monster a face and a name had taken away some of *its* power. Turning her face toward God had given *her* power. She had so much to heal from, so much work to do, but she wanted to do it the right way this time, not through sheer willpower, but with God...and with Noah.

She'd have to go back to North Carolina and dig into Keith Galloway's murder case with her team. She wanted to see that through to the end, but still...

She was Noah's. He was hers. And after she returned home, they'd be all in, together.

Kelsie held up her hand, and he slid the ring onto her finger.

She glanced at it then rose to kiss him again, pulling him close and promising him forever.

\* \* \* \* \*

*If you enjoyed this
Trinity Investigative Team book
by Jodie Bailey,
pick up these previous titles in the miniseries*

Taken at Christmas
Protecting the Orphan

*Available now from Love Inspired Suspense!*

Dear Reader,

I won't lie, Kelsie's story was tough to write. Our stories can be difficult, and it can be hard to balance our pain with God's grace, mercy and love. It can be tough to understand why bad things happen. We walk different paths, feel different feelings, and endure different trials.

Sometimes, in the midst of our pain, the truth can feel like a cliché. Kelsie's story is delicate, and I never wanted it to be a cliché. I wanted to honor those who have walked her rocky, treacherous path. I wanted them to feel seen and to realize that healing is there. If Kelsie's story is similar to yours, you can find someone to talk to at RAINN.org. You don't have to be alone.

It can be difficult to see God sometimes. One thing I've learned is that He is always there, although sometimes I can't see Him until I'm out of the darkest valley and looking back. Also, as Kelsie learned, when you hand bad things to Him, He uses them to help someone else. As Val said, there are times we can sit with someone in their pain because we've been there first. Our pain, our struggles, can become hard-won victories we get to share with others. It's not easy, but it's one of the gifts that comes from trusting Jesus. Our God is good even when our circumstances aren't. I pray that you will come to know that.

# Get up to 4 Free Books!

### We'll send you 2 free books from each series you try PLUS a free Mystery Gift.

**FREE Value Over $25**

Both the **Love Inspired®** and **Love Inspired® Suspense** series feature compelling novels filled with inspirational romance, faith, forgiveness and hope.

---

**YES!** Please send me 2 FREE novels from the Love Inspired or Love Inspired Suspense series and my FREE gift (gift is worth about $10 retail). After receiving them, if I don't wish to receive any more books, I can return the shipping statement marked "cancel." If I don't cancel, I will receive 6 brand-new Love Inspired Larger-Print books or Love Inspired Suspense Larger-Print books every month and be billed just $7.19 each in the U.S. or $7.99 each in Canada. That is a savings of 20% off the cover price. It's quite a bargain! Shipping and handling is just 50¢ per book in the U.S. and $1.25 per book in Canada.* I understand that accepting the 2 free books and gift places me under no obligation to buy anything. I can always return a shipment and cancel at any time by calling the number below. The free books and gift are mine to keep no matter what I decide.

Choose one:
- ☐ **Love Inspired Larger-Print** (122/322 BPA G36Y)
- ☐ **Love Inspired Suspense Larger-Print** (107/307 BPA G36Y)
- ☐ **Or Try Both!** (122/322 & 107/307 BPA G36Z)

Name (please print)

Address                                                                                      Apt. #

City                                 State/Province                                Zip/Postal Code

**Email:** Please check this box ☐ if you would like to receive newsletters and promotional emails from Harlequin Enterprises ULC and its affiliates. You can unsubscribe anytime.

### Mail to the Harlequin Reader Service:
**IN U.S.A.:** P.O. Box 1341, Buffalo, NY 14240-8531
**IN CANADA:** P.O. Box 603, Fort Erie, Ontario L2A 5X3

Want to explore our other series or interested in ebooks? Visit www.ReaderService.com or call 1-800-873-8635.

---

*Terms and prices subject to change without notice. Prices do not include sales taxes, which will be charged (if applicable) based on your state or country of residence. Canadian residents will be charged applicable taxes. Offer not valid in Quebec. This offer is limited to one order per household. Books received may not be as shown. Not valid for current subscribers to the Love Inspired or Love Inspired Suspense series. All orders subject to approval. Credit or debit balances in a customer's account(s) may be offset by any other outstanding balance owed by or to the customer. Please allow 4 to 6 weeks for delivery. Offer available while quantities last.

**Your Privacy**—Your information is being collected by Harlequin Enterprises ULC, operating as Harlequin Reader Service. For a complete summary of the information we collect, how we use this information and to whom it is disclosed, please visit our privacy notice located at https://corporate.harlequin.com/privacy-notice. Notice to California Residents – Under California law, you have specific rights to control and access your data. For more information on these rights and how to exercise them, visit https://corporate.harlequin.com/california-privacy. For additional information for residents of other U.S. states that provide their residents with certain rights with respect to personal data, visit https://corporate.harlequin.com/other-state-residents-privacy-rights/.

LIRLIS25